LETTERS OF
Forgiveness

LETTERS OF
Forgiveness

A NOVEL

CATHY SCHAFFER

O'LEARY PUBLISHING
The Influencer's Press

BONITA SPRINGS, FL

ISBN 978-1-7341589-1-5 (Print)
ISBN 978-1-7341589-2-2 (eBook)
Library of Congress Control Number: 2019917620

Book Design by Jessica Angerstein
Photography by Julie Renner Photography
Editing by Heather Davis Desrocher
Line Editing by Matthew Acton

Printed in the United States of America

This story is dedicated to all those who have gone before us.
Let us learn from their history.

CONTENTS

So often times it happens that we live our lives in chains
And we never even know we have the key.

"Already Gone" by the Eagles

PROLOGUE

I hate war as only a soldier who has lived it can, only as one who has seen its brutality, its futility, its stupidity.

—DWIGHT D. EISENHOWER

KANDAHAR, AFGHANISTAN
DECEMBER 31, 2012
0000 HOURS

The rotors of the big Chinook helicopter stirred up the talcum-powder-like dust of the Kandahar desert as it slowed to land, creating a surreal effect on the desert's moonscape likeness. Departing from the helicopter, the team appeared as shadowy figures rising from the screen of dust and lights and disappeared like ghosts as they walked into the darkness. This was the routine. First, Army Rangers led the team in and secured the area, then the Cultural Support Team (CST) followed, quickly, behind them. Twenty-four-year-old Second Lieutenant Kathryn Glass, known to everyone as Katy, was the lead on the CST, a veteran of fifteen encounters since arriving in Kandahar seven months earlier. Joining her on this mission were her interpreter and best friend, Shveta Mohamer; the MEDEVAC medical crew, which included her lover, Lieutenant Commander Jack Foster; and her captain and his elite force of Army Rangers.

"Should be an easy run," Katy shouted at Shveta over the roar of the helicopter.

Two hours prior to departing, Katy had run over the checklist for the gear she would need with the supply sergeant. "Helmet, night goggles, headset for communication, M4 rifle, M9 pistol," she said out loud as she received each item. "Hey, Gunny, how about a little ammunition for these things?" she reminded him as she held up the weapons.

Shaking his head, he sighed and said, "Yes, ma'am, got it right here" and handed her multiple rounds of ammo for the guns.

He still doesn't get us girls, she thought to herself and smiled. Katy continued collecting the rest of her equipment—eye protection, nutrition bars, water, latex gloves, and tourniquets for possible injuries—her checklist was complete. Then, she and the other team members sat through a mission briefing that took place an hour prior to leaving.

Jumping from the helicopter, Katy swore silently as she landed wrong and twisted her ankle. *Damn desert rocks!* She was 115 pounds, five feet, three inches tall, and carried eighty pounds of gear and Kevlar, standard gear for anyone on the front lines of war. Because of the brownout caused by the helicopter rotors, she had to stop for a minute to adjust her night vision goggles. Through the eerie green light of her goggles, she located the men about fifty feet in front of her. Her ankle hurt, but she still made the short run to the village with Shveta by her side. She was careful to avoid any further mutant rocks, animal burrows, or mine craters. These were constant hazards in the darkness of Kandahar.

Arriving at the edge of the village, with the helicopter just within visual range and the medics on full alert, Katy and Shveta waited for the all-clear from the captain. As they waited, Katy remarked to Shveta, "The temperature is comfortable tonight. I was absolutely freezing last night. I guess it's that time of year."

Shveta nodded her head in acknowledgment and grinned.

"OK, Glass, it looks like you're good to go. Go do your magic," Katy heard through her headset.

She smiled as she nodded at Shveta, and they walked together toward an area where the village women were gathered.

As Katy approached the group of women, she noticed the Rangers darting about out of the corner of her eye. *That's odd,* she thought. *What are they doing?* She immediately pulled Shveta to her side and slowed her pace. Katy was listening to her radio headset for further information when she heard the sharp crack of a pistol. Then all hell broke loose.

"Kandahar base, we are under attack. Insurgents firing . . ." was the last thing Katy heard the captain say over the headset.

Katy saw the first explosion as if it were in slow motion. Someone had stepped on a daisy chain and set off a series of linked IEDs. As the second explosion occurred, Shveta shrieked and ran for the helicopter before Katy could stop her. Yelling at her to stop, Katy watched Shveta deviate from their original path. But, it was too late. Shveta stepped on another hidden pressure plate, setting off an explosive. Katy watched in horror as Shveta was blown to pieces by the IED. As her Kevlar was splattered with small pieces of Shveta's body parts, Katy let out a primal, gut-wrenching scream, "Shveta!" The horror she had just witnessed froze her in place. It was as if she weighed a thousand pounds and couldn't move. Finally, Katy's brain registered what was happening and a split second later, sent a message telling her muscles to move.

"Kandahar, Kandahar, this is Red Company. We are under attack, chain IEDs activated. Captain dead, multiple wounded. Will MEDEVAC as soon as safe." The conversation crackled through Katy's headset from the helicopter.

The village women started to run in the opposite direction, and Katy yelled out to the women in an attempt to stop them, worried they were headed for more buried IEDs. When they didn't stop and no further IEDs went off in their direction, Katy turned toward the helicopter. She saw Jack waving his arms at her from the helicopter's bay when he suddenly jumped down and started running toward her. She screamed at him, "Jack, stop!"

But it was too late. another IED exploded twenty feet from him, and he was thrown into the air like a rag doll. Katy froze as he landed on the ground with a heavy thud.

"Oh my God. No, no, no! Not here! No! No! No!" Bullets flying by her head forced her to drop and body crawl over to Jack's bloodied and shattered corpse. The shrapnel wound to his head had been fatal. Heart pounding and adrenaline rushing, she pulled his lifeless body close to her dust-covered fatigues as if to protect him from any further harm as bullets zipped by her head and mines exploded nearby. Tracers and their pyrotechnic charges lit up the night sky, illuminating his lifeless blue eyes, and, in her terror and shock, Katy was sure she was going to die.

PART 1

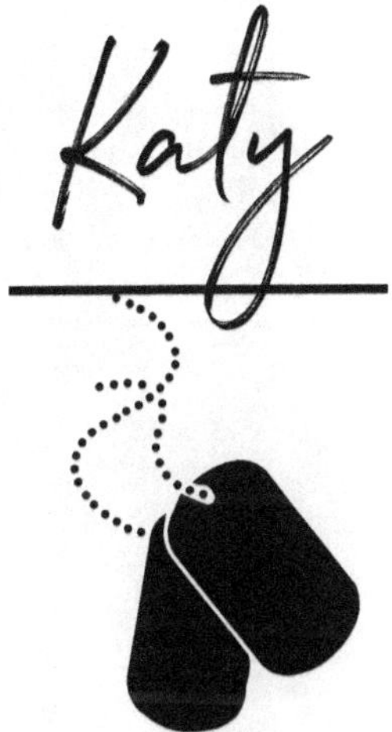

CHAPTER I

Not all women wear pearls and sensible shoes to work,
some wear dog tags and combat boots.

—UNKNOWN

Someone yelled, "Atten-shun!"

The group immediately stopped what they were doing, fell into formation, and came to full attention. Katy saw her commander approaching.

"Commander!" Katy saluted.

Returning the salute, he said, "Second Lieutenant Glass, you are to report to my office at 1400 hours."

"Sir, yes sir," she replied.

The commander did an about-face and walked away.

Wow, I wonder what that's all about, Katy thought. Returning to her troops, she finished their drills and then ran over to the commander's office. With a blonde ponytail bobbing from underneath her patrol cap and a muscular frame belying her petite stature, Katy crossed the quad without effort. Intense brown eyes peered out above high cheekbones and an angular jawline. Her full lips were pursed, giving her a look of authority, but, when she relaxed, they were full and sensuous.

Entering the office, she found the Commander speaking to his secretary. Katy came to attention and said, "Second Lieutenant Glass reporting as ordered, sir."

He looked up and, with a nod of his head, indicated that Katy should follow him into his office.

"Close the door, Glass."

"Yes, sir."

Once the door was closed and he was sitting behind his desk, he became slightly less formal. "Katy, sit down."

Katy took a seat in front of his desk.

"Katy, you are an extremely talented individual, and your services to this company have been exemplary." His voice softened. "But, Katy, I know you're restless. So," he sighed, "this came across my desk this morning, and I think it's something you would be well qualified for." He handed her a flyer.

Letters of Forgiveness

The flyer immediately caught her attention. On it was a photo of a female officer crouching with an M4 assault rifle in her hands. The headline read:

FEMALE SOLDIERS BECOME A PART OF HISTORY!

She looked up at the commander and back down at the flyer.

"Katy, this is a new program that the military is giving a trial run. With your communication skills and physical abilities, you are exactly what they need. You would be part of Special Ops with the Army Rangers on the front lines. They desperately need women like you. Take the flyer, go do some research, and let me know if you want me to recommend you for the program. It won't be easy to qualify . . .I hear the physical requirements are a bear, so be prepared. But as for intelligence, communication, being a team player—you've got it made. Any questions?"

"Umm, no sir. Thank you, sir," Katy said, quite surprised.

"Dismissed, Second Lieutenant."

Katy did an about-face and left the office with the flyer in hand. As soon as she was out of the commander's office, she took off for her quarters at a run, her adrenaline-fueled by her excitement. Katy knew the commander did not give compliments easily, and he was certainly not one to give up personnel. So, this had to be special. Ever since she was a little girl, Katy had visions of doing something big, bold, and adventurous. It seemed as if her entire life had been leading her to this moment.

Kathryn Margaret Glass was born into the Hollywood elite. Her father was a very successful Hollywood producer, and her mother came from Texas oil. A tough-minded businessman, her father believed in hard work, self-discipline, and the American dream. He also had an artistic nature that showed in his photography and his ability to recognize profitable movie projects. Her mother was his exact opposite. Soft-hearted, nurturing, and athletic, she had carried the most influence with Katy. Both of her parents had fostered an independent streak in her and insisted that Katy follow her own path. The only rules were to maintain good grades in school and to have an after-school job when she wasn't participating in extracurricular athletics.

Katy did it all. She worked at the local drugstore as a cashier and became an outstanding track and field athlete, as well as an accomplished soccer player. She shared her mother's altruistic heart and spent many hours after school volunteering for various causes and fundraisers. In her sophomore year, she raised five thousand dollars for the local food bank. In school, she had a reputation as someone with a strong commitment to helping others. That commitment and her athletic ability won her a scholarship to UC Berkeley. It seemed as if there wasn't a challenge that Katy couldn't meet.

At Berkeley, Katy enrolled in the Communications program and, while there, much to her parents' chagrin, joined the Army ROTC program. Katy loved the highly structured environment and physical challenges of ROTC. Meeting deadlines, tight schedules, and working by the book appealed to her highly organized personality. The Army also fulfilled her need to live a life of service. During her ROTC program, she won several medals for marksmanship, physical training, and communications. After graduating at the top of her class, the Army sent her to Fort Bragg to begin her stint as a Defense Information Specialist.

Her Communications degree allowed her to integrate seamlessly into the Army's Defense Information Program (DIP), and she decided to become a war correspondent. She was intrigued by and in awe of the women who made up the long history of her chosen profession. Every night, Katy looked over a little notebook she kept in her bedside table where she kept a list of female war correspondents who impressed her. Her list reminded her that she was joining a special sisterhood. These brave women had paved the way and provided her with inspiration and determination. She took great pleasure in the knowledge that someday she might join this prestigious list of names.

Frederika Charlotte Riedesel, whose letters and memoirs relating to the Revolutionary War and the capture of the German troops at Saratoga began a long line of female war correspondents.

Kate Adie, a British journalist with assignments in the Gulf War, the war in the former Socialist Federal Republic of Yugoslavia, the Rwandan genocide, and the Sierra Leone Civil War.

Margaret Bourke-White, the first female war correspondent to photograph the Buchenwald concentration camp.

Dickey Chapelle, who had the dubious honor of being the first female war correspondent killed in action.

Gloria Emerson, author of Winners and Losers based on her experience covering the Vietnam War for the New York Times between 1970 and 1972.

Georgie Anne Geyer, the first Western reporter to interview Saddam Hussein in 1973. She was also held by authorities in Angola for writing reports on that country's civil war.

Clare Hollingworth, covered World War II, the Algerian War, the Vietnam War, and the Bangladesh Liberation

War of 1971. Her eyewitness account was the first report the British Foreign Office received about the German invasion of Poland. She reportedly held her phone outside her window so the consulate could hear the sounds of the massive troop movement.

Helen Kirkpatrick, covered the Blitz, the Normandy Invasion, and the Liberation of France.

Katy Webb, covered the Vietnam and Cambodian wars for UPI. She was captured by the North Vietnamese in Cambodia in 1971 and contributed a chapter to War Torn that described her experiences in captivity. She later covered East Timor, The Gulf War, Indonesia, and Afghanistan for AFP.

Marie Colvin, covered the conflicts in Syria, Sierra Leone, Chechnya, Sri Lanka, and Libya. She was killed while on assignment in Homs, Syria.

Christiane Amanpour, a major voice in the coverage of the Iran-Iraq war who also provided coverage of the Bosnian Civil War and the persecution of Muslims in Sarajevo.

Katy immersed herself in her DIP studies with her usual fervor and dedication. When her training was completed, she was assigned to the Fort Bragg PR division and, once there, became very quickly bored. Being a base correspondent officer was not the adventure she had envisioned for her life. Writing stories about base life and PR for the company rapidly became a chore she did not look forward to. She secretly envied those who were deployed to the Middle East. She longed for a chance to do something of substance, and the commander had just opened a door to that possibility. So, immediately after the meeting with her commander, she went online to research the Cultural Support program.

The wars in Iraq and Afghanistan were changing traditional military operations. No longer were men lining up in formation to fight with their guns and tanks. This war was staged inside villages and in the streets. It was a war of concealment and surprise attacks. Insurgents acted like marauders and conducted surprise raids, coming out of nowhere. This was not a strategy the military had faced since the wars with the Native Americans back in the 1700s and 1800s. Insurgents, many of them nihilists acting in the name of religion, were a treacherous and poorly understood enemy.

Technology had radically altered the battlefield as well, but military officials knew the soldiers on the ground were being deprived of "micro-knowledge," a firsthand look into the region's people, culture, language, and social customs. This was the intelligence needed to thwart terrorism and insurgency.

Senior military brass believed that Middle Eastern women were the critical missing link.

For centuries, Muslim women were seen as the figurehead for family honor within the religion. Preserving sexual chastity among women in the family was the responsibility of male family members. Upon reaching adolescence, and until their marriage, women's faces were never seen by any non-related male, only by male family members or other women. Forbidden to leave the family home without a male escort, they were required to wear a chadri or burqa to completely cover their faces in public. But, these women were in a position to see and hear many things because they were virtually invisible to the male population. Military officials wanted access to this repository of knowledge.

But, every time a male soldier caught a glimpse of a Muslim woman's face, the military lost what some called "vital human terrain." Violating this tradition, a foundation of Muslim society, caused larger issues than just the loss of life. Garnering support for counterinsurgency efforts became more difficult due to these encroachments on the region's culture. Building wells and septic systems, schools, and new government infrastructures helped convince locals to move away from insurgency and enhance their loyalty to the United States. But, whenever a soldier interrogated a Muslim female or searched her quarters, the military took two steps backwards in establishing crucial influential ground. Unfortunately, a directive limiting that type of engagement meant troops were unable to search women's quarters or the women themselves, a perilous situation for the men on the ground. Insurgents escaped detection by hiding their weapons in the quarters of Muslim women or, worse yet, by dressing like females.

Initially, the concept of female interrogators had been operationalized by an impromptu group of female Marines located on Iraqi military bases. Drivers, mechanics, and information officers volunteered to interrogate and obtain information from village women. But, it soon became apparent that these women lacked necessary on-the-ground tactical training, and most of them were improvising in their new roles. This put the women and their teams in grave danger. When mayhem erupted, it was essential that the teams be combat-ready and tactically trained.

So, the U.S. military finally decided to develop an all-female team that could assist frontline troops by interacting with Afghani and Iraqi women, as well as their children. The Cultural Support Team would open communications with the female Muslim population. Women with highly specialized communication skills who were combat-trained soldiers would attach to Special Operation Forces, the elite servicemen of the Army and Marine Corps. Attaching these women to tactical units also allowed the military to legally bypass the ban on women assigned to frontline warfare.

I can't believe it, Katy thought. *It's like this program was made just for me!* She jumped up from her desk and started pacing. *This is an opportunity of a lifetime. I can serve, explore a place I've never been to, and possibly be a part of military history*, she thought. "I want this!" she said out loud as she slammed her hand down on her desk. The next morning, she was back in the commander's office.

CHAPTER 11

Love can defeat that nameless terror.
Loving one another, we take the sting from death.

—EDWARD ABBEY

FORT BRAGG, NC
JANUARY 2012

Six weeks after first speaking to her commander, Katy found herself in the lobby of a local inn near Fort Bragg surrounded by a diverse group of highly fit military women of various ages, ethnicities, and backgrounds. All were awaiting further instructions as they began the assessment and selection portion of the Cultural Support Team (CST) training. *Wow,* Katy thought, *these women are monsters. Look at that one over there. She could pick up two of me.* Coffee flowed freely, and conversation that started as a low-level buzz escalated into loud, jubilant exchanges. Katy grabbed a bowl of cereal and a glass of juice and found a table. As she sat down, she introduced herself to her tablemates, who reciprocated in kind. Katy sensed the level of competition among the women was extremely high, but there was also a feeling of camaraderie among them. Every single woman in the group knew that whoever was chosen for this assignment was going to make history and change the way women were viewed in the military. Every single woman in the room wanted this thing to succeed.

Still, no one anticipated the grueling mental and physical training that the women applying for assignment to the CST unit would endure. This new program was designed to recruit the best of the best. Physical conditioning, thinking under duress, and communications were the three components that formed the basis of every training session. Twenty-mile hikes carrying eighty pounds of gear and Kevlar through the swamps of North Carolina challenged even the strongest women. An obstacle course demanded strength and determination as they climbed ropes without using their legs and crawled through mud under barbwire trying to make time. After their late-night hikes, they were often called to formation and required to stand in the summer heat in full gear while they received a lecture about Middle Eastern history. Katy's will and athleticism served her well during this time. Calling on her memories of training for state championships in track and field, she powered through the toughest obstacle courses by putting one foot in front of the other. Her written test scores were always at or above the 90th percentile. She won the respect of many of the women competing for spots on the CST because of her resolute will, determination, and extraordinary effort.

On the last day of training, the group was assigned a long-distance hike. It was raining in sheets as they started the twenty-mile swamp hike carrying eighty pounds of gear while wearing Kevlar, with only a compass and a map to guide them through the North Carolina backwoods. They were to be timed individually. This was the final test before Phase 2 of the program. Making her way through the heavy underbrush and vines, Katy smiled as she was reminded of a song she liked as a little girl by Johnny Horton called The Battle of New Orleans.

They ran through the briar and they ran through the bramble,
And they ran through the bushes where a rabbit wouldn't go,
They ran so fast that the hounds couldn't catch them,
Down the Mississippi to the Gulf of Mexico.

The cadence of the song kept her moving at a pretty good clip. But, about ten miles in, she came across a woman she knew as Lynette. Katy was Lynette's senior officer, but she didn't know her very well. Lynette was tall and lanky, and she had a reputation for being aloof and a loner. Katy knew she was not well liked by some of her peers. Lynette had stumbled and twisted her ankle in some unseen hole and now she was sitting on the ground, trying to wrap her ankle with an elastic bandage.

Katy stopped and asked, "Soldier, you OK?"

"Yes ma'am, I just need to wrap my ankle."

"How badly are you hurt?"

"It's pretty bad, but I'm going to make it no matter what. I just might be late for dinner." Lynette smiled, tears running down her face.

Katy knew if Lynette was the last to arrive, no matter what difficulty she was facing, she would be eliminated from Phase 2 selection.

Without hesitation, Katy said, "Tell you what, soldier, no one's going to call you late for dinner. We'll do it together, all right?"

Lynette looked at Katy in disbelief as Katy took the bandage, wrapped her ankle, and then lifted Lynette's pack from her back.

"Ma'am, you can't carry everything—"

"You let me worry about that, soldier," Katy said, and they were off. It was incredibly slow going after that. Soaked by the rain and sucking mud, they limped and slid along. But, Katy forged on with Lynette's arm around one shoulder and her pack on the other arm. They crawled up mud-slick hills, pushing the packs and themselves up inch by inch. Eventually, they came across two other candidates. Dripping with sweat and covered with muck, they looked as if they had been mud wrestling. Katy's arm hurt from carrying Lynette's eighty-pound pack, but all she said was, "Anyone got any Advil?"

The comment and the sight of the two women had everyone laughing, and they sat for a breather. Lynette told the story of how Katy had come to her rescue despite knowing she was ruining her chances of getting picked.

Katy just shook her head. "That's not what matters, soldier."

As Katy and Lynette got back up to leave, the other two women insisted on helping them as well. One of them took Lynette's pack, and the other gave Katy a breather by letting Lynette lean on her. It was dark by the time the foursome got back to camp, but they had forged a bond between them that they would never forget. As far as Katy was concerned, this was what military unity was all about.

When they got back, Katy eyed the deserted quad and asked, "Do you think there's any food left?"

As expected, the kitchen was closed up tighter than a drum. So they made do with a couple of items from the snack machines and hit the sack.

The next day, they were called to formation by the unit commander. They would all learn their fates that morning, as the recruits selected for Phase 2 were to be announced.

"At ease, soldiers," the commander began. "As you know, we've been watching all of you very carefully, looking for the crème de la crème, as it were. You are some of the military's finest recruits, and all of you have displayed exemplary attitudes and outstanding physical aptitudes. But as you all know, only fifteen of you will be chosen here this morning. But before we make that announcement, there is some business to attend to. Second Lieutenant Glass, front and center!" he commanded.

Katy marched up to the commander, came to attention, and saluted.

"Second Lieutenant, did you understand the rules of yesterday's engagement?"

Feeling a bit nervous, Katy said, "Sir, yes, I did, sir."

"Second Lieutenant, you understood that you were being timed and that to be picked for a spot on the CST, you needed to have a record time?"

Katy felt a lump in her throat and her stomach tightened. She had known that stopping to help Lynette was going to cost her, but now she was going to pay the price in front of everyone. "Sir, yes sir!" she said, swallowing hard and trying to control her breathing.

"Very well then, Second Lieutenant, at ease." The commander turned to address the larger group. "This morning at 0800 hours, a report was made to me of four recruits' delayed arrival back to base following yesterday's assignment. The details included in the report noted selfless behavior, assisting a wounded soldier, and procuring the needed assistance to get everyone back to base intact." Looking at Katy, he went on. "Second Lieutenant, your actions and behavior are exactly what this Army needs in its recruits. Your notable sacrifice for your teammate is the attitude we want for the CST units. I want to recognize you as the first candidate selected to go on to Phase 2. Second Lieutenant, you are a credit to the service," he said, reaching out and shaking Katy's hand. "Congratulations," he smiled. "Dismissed!"

As Katy returned to her place in formation, the whole group erupted into loud applause. Tears welled up in her eyes. Katy knew every one of the women in formation was the best of the best the Army had to offer, and each had given a 110 percent of their energy and knowledge to this project. Katy thought, *they all deserve that applause.* The other three women who had been delayed with Katy were also selected to move on to Phase 2.

CHAPTER III

Beware of wolves in sheep's clothing.

—MATTHEW 7:15

FORT BRAGG, NC
MARCH 2012

Phase 2 entailed training for the missions she would be assigned to in less than three months. During that time, her team nicknamed her "Little Tiger." She laughed every time someone called her that. Despite her petite size, Katy came to be known as a force to be reckoned with.

As a young girl, Katy had enjoyed playing with the boys more than with the other girls. Climbing trees, playing hide and seek, smoking cigarettes behind the garage (for a very brief time), and hanging out with boys after school had earned Katy the tomboy label. It wasn't so much that she wanted to be a boy.

It was just that boys always seemed to have much more fun than girls. Besides, running, soccer, basketball, and competing just seemed natural to her. She loved how her body felt when it moved and stretched beyond physical norms. In high school, her physical strength and athletic abilities had defined her. Those skills certainly helped her breeze through ROTC's physical requirements. There were only a few women who could do a one-arm pull-up immediately upon entrance, and she was one of them.

After three months of some of the most grueling physical and mental preparation and testing the Army could dish out, Katy successfully passed and was admitted to the elite group of women known as the Cultural Support Team. Her first assignment, Kandahar, Afghanistan.

Calling her parents to tell them she was going to Afghanistan was like starting World War III.

"Daddy, I have something important to tell you," Katy began. She had purposefully kept all information about what she was doing hidden from her parents. She had not wanted their protests to interfere with her concentration during the selection process.

"Daddy, I'm leaving for Afghanistan in two weeks," she nervously told him over the phone. She was more than willing to stand up to monstrous insurgents, but telling her father she was headed to Kandahar was the scariest thing she had ever done.

"What . . . Katy . . . I don't understand . . . how . . . why . . . why are you going to Afghanistan?" he asked, his voice deep with concern and surprise.

"Daddy, I was chosen to be part of a new elite group of women called CSTs. We are going to help change the direction of the war in the Middle East," she said, trying to make sure he understood there were others like her as well. "Daddy, this is a chance for me to be a part of history."

"I don't give a damn if it's your chance to be the president, young lady. You will not be going to Afghanistan!" he exploded. He threatened to call every senator he knew and then said he would drag her kicking and screaming back to California. Katy knew it was going to be a difficult conversation, but she hadn't expected him to threaten to intervene in her decision.

She called home several times over the next two weeks, but her father refused to talk to her. Her mother just cried every time she called and begged her to come home.

"Mom, stop. Please, just stop. I'm going. Can you please just wish me luck? I promise I'll write often and let you know where I am. As much as I can," Katy told her mother on her last call home before her deployment. "Mom, please . . . " she whispered into the phone.

Katy heard her mother slowly compose herself over the phone. Her mother offered up a couple of sighs of resignation and then said, "I love you, my brave soldier. You come back to me safely, Katy, do you hear me? Be safe, honey."

In the end, her father never did say goodbye. Katy was hurt but not surprised. Perhaps it was just too hard to say goodbye to his little girl, or maybe he just didn't want to admit defeat. Whatever the case, Katy was thoroughly surprised when she received his letter at mail call a month after her arrival.

My Dearest Katy,

I hope this finds you safe, warm, and dry. I'm not sure what it's like there in Afghanistan. When I was in Vietnam, it was all we ever thought about. Staying dry, that is. Did I ever tell you that I spent time in 'Nam? I was a war correspondent, but I was assigned by the magazine I worked for. It was the start of my career. I won several awards for photojournalism during my time there. But the horrors that I witnessed in that war tainted those awards for me. I barely made it out of there alive when Saigon crashed.

I wanted you to know this so you might understand why I was so upset with your decision. I guess I'm still trying to protect my "little girl."

But you are a big girl now, a beautiful young woman, actually, with a life of her own. I was wrong not to come and say goodbye to you when you left. I will live with that regret for the rest of my life. But know this. I love you. You are following in your old man's footsteps for better or worse, and I couldn't be prouder. I am so sorry I acted like an ass when you left. I hope you will forgive me. You are, and always will be, my little Katy. Please write and tell me everything that is happening over there.

Come home safely, Katy.

Love,

Dad

Katy felt a lump in her throat and tears welling up in her eyes as she read his letter. It was an uncharacteristically emotional letter from her father, and it left her with many questions. *My father was in Vietnam? He never said a word. Why didn't Mom tell me? He was a correspondent? Wow!* She tried to imagine her father in fatigues in the jungles of Vietnam but couldn't. She tried to see if she could find any of his work online. Unfortunately, internet service was limited and censored on base, and she was unable to find anything he wrote. But, in the meantime, the newfound understanding that came from reading her father's letter touched her, and she found herself quite emotional that day.

Thankfully, she was off duty the day his letter arrived. After reading it, she wandered aimlessly around base trying to get a grip on her emotions. Katy had arrived in Kandahar in mid-May and had felt homesick for the last few days. Reading her father's letter exacerbated those feelings of sadness and isolation. She tried distracting herself in the movie theater, but she couldn't sit still. After the aborted attempt to watch a movie, she decided to find a quiet spot in the corner of the little cafe on base. She was completely absorbed in her coffee and thoughts when a tall figure stopped at her table.

"Second Lieutenant," a man said gently, "everything all right?"

Katy had not seen him approach, and when she saw the lieutenant commander, she about fell out of her chair trying to stand up and come to attention.

"Sorry, sir! I didn't see you coming, I was . . . .was . . . um . . . just um . . . thinking!" she said as she stood at attention.

"At ease, Second Lieutenant, at ease. Sit down. Please!" he said with a smile. "I just couldn't help noticing the faraway look on your face. We see that a lot here, especially in our new troops. As experienced officers, we're supposed to offer support and advice to our new people. You just looked like you could use some . . . support and advice."

"Thank you for your concern, Lieutenant Commander. I got a letter from home that touched an emotional nerve, I guess, and it's been on my mind all day. Really, I'm fine."

"I know how that can be," he said, smiling. "May I join you?"

Surprised by his request, Katy said, "Yes, of course."

Lieutenant Commander Jack Foster was part of the Army medical service and served as the company's Master Flight Surgeon. As they sat together, he told Katy that he had accrued seven years of service so far and had been deployed to Afghanistan several times over the years. "Went home for a brief period and then redeployed here, to Kandahar," he told Katy. His relaxed manner and soft voice allowed easy conversation to flow between them.

Katy thought he looked young for all of his experience, but then she noticed the fine lines around his eyes and the slight touch of gray in his hair. He had electric blue eyes with just a hint of the devil in them. *His smile could light up a room*, she thought.

Their conversation that day moved on to family. He had been adopted as a child. He did not know his biological parents but spoke fondly of his adopted parents. "They were devoted parents. I will be eternally grateful for all they gave me." He'd lost both of them in a horrible car accident four years ago.

He went to college on a football scholarship to the University of Alabama. As the starting quarterback, he suffered a knee injury that cost him the position on the team and his scholarship. So, he drifted for a while doing odd jobs. He returned to his parents' home for a short time, but his father insisted he find a way to support himself. So Jack turned to the Army.

Army tuition assistance put him through undergrad and then medical school. Once he had completed school, he worked his way up the ranks through hard work, intellect, and multiple deployments. He'd arrived in Kandahar as a Master Flight Surgeon about four months prior to Katy's arrival. As the MEDEVAC staff team leader, he went out on missions to provide immediate medical attention to troops in the field. "Every once in a while, I have to pick up a gun and shoot alongside the boys," he said, "but I don't like it. It messes with your head."

For two hours they talked as if they were old friends, laughing and trading life stories. Katy described how she came to be one of the newest members of the Cultural Support Team and how honored she was to be a part of this moment in military history. Jack acknowledged her enthusiasm but warned her, "It's dangerous out there." By the time they were done talking, Katy had forgotten about the raw emotions sparked by her father's letter.

"Second Lieutenant, I hope our little chat has helped," he said as he stood to leave.

"Yes sir! Thank you for your time. I'm sure I will see you around the base." She stood to present her very best Army salute.

"Second Lieutenant!" he returned the salute and left.

Katy watched him walk out and couldn't help noticing the muscular build under his uniform. *Wow! He's a hunk*, she thought with a smile.

—

Over the next three weeks, the weather in Kandahar started to heat up, but Katy barely noticed. She was occupied with her new routine and learning about her new teammates. One of the first people she met was Shveta Mohamer. Shveta was the interpreter for Katy's CST team. She was fluent in both Pashto and Dari, the two most common languages spoken in Afghanistan. She had grown up in Kandahar, a daughter of progressive Muslim parents. Katy thought she was beautiful with her long black hair, olive skin, and deep green eyes that peered out from the traditional hijab she wore around her head. She was petite, like Katy, but not as physically strong. Shveta had attended Kandahar University and had been awarded the equivalent of a bachelor's degree in communications and Middle Eastern studies. Contracted as a civilian interpreter by the Army, she was very good at her job. She was in her first six months at Kandahar when Katy met her. Shveta was smart, energetic, savvy, and easy to be around, and she and Katy hit it off instantly.

"Stick with me, Katy, and I'll show you around the base. And, I can tell you who to watch out for and who you need to know," Shveta said at their first meeting.

"OK, Shveta, I'm all yours because I'm totally lost right now," Katy replied, smiling.

Shveta had a knack for purposely making male troops squirm. "As a minority gender, Katy, you learn to be on the offensive just to avoid getting embarrassed. For instance, let's say you need tampons and you know you have to go to the PX to get them. There's one of our guys, a big bruiser, behind the counter. So, you're thinking, 'Ugh, I don't want to ask him for tampons.' But instead of acting all shy and embarrassed, you have to walk up to the guy, look him square in the eyes, and in the most serious voice you can muster, say, 'I need some tampons,'" Shveta said with a devious smile. "Then you wait. Never let your eyes leave his eyes first and watch how many shades of red the big guy can turn. The trick is to not flinch first when you ask for them," she said, laughing.

Katy found her good humor infectious and quite unusual. Shveta was Katy's constant companion at all the briefings and drills that comprised life in Kandahar. When it came time for Katy's first mission, it was Shveta who showed her the way, demonstrating the behavior necessary to engage and complete a mission. It was Shveta who showed Katy how to adjust her night-vision goggles and how to traverse desert terrain at night. "You have to watch out for those miserable small desert rocks that can twist your ankle and bring you to the ground in a second," Shveta warned. Katy was immensely relieved to have Shveta as her mentor and friend. Life on base became less lonely as their friendship evolved.

As one of the junior officers, Katy had other duties as well. Gaining confidence and credibility, she began to internalize personal accountability for her soldiers. *Keep the boys alive* was her singular conviction of responsibility. Because of her commitment to her unit troops, she won over many and became well liked and respected on base. There were also times when she was assigned to convoys as a turret gunner. She did not particularly enjoy being a turret gunner because it was a hot and sweaty position within the Humvees, but she told herself this was another way that she could ensure the safety of her men. She handled the M60 machine gun as well as any man, and when it came time to use it, she was a lethal shot. Her gung-ho spirit and energy were contagious, and Katy became known as the go-to person if something needed to be accomplished in her unit.

Life on base slowly became more comfortable and predictable. She noticed she was constantly running into Jack Foster. At first, she thought it very odd that, despite her grueling schedule, he always seemed to be around the corner, in the cafeteria, or somewhere nearby. Initially, he just smiled and waved whenever he saw her. But as the weeks passed, he became more friendly and familiar, putting his long arm around her shoulders to make a joke or comment before moving on. He made her feel secure in this strange place so far away from home.

One sweltering night, after a particularly long day, Katy and Shveta went to the base cafe to order iced coffees in an attempt to ward off the heat. They were sitting at the cafe bar when Jack walked in.

"Ladies, can I get you a drink?" he asked with a huge smile on his face.

"Lieutenant Commander, why the big smile?" Shveta asked, brushing off his question.

"Well, ma'am, to tell you the truth, I love finding beautiful women in a hell hole like this. It gives me hope that beauty prevails," he said with a big grin and hint of a tease in his voice.

"Uh-oh, sounds like a pick-up line to me, Katy," Shveta said, shrugging her shoulders and looking at Katy. "We better be careful, or he'll try to smooth talk us right into his quarters."

Katy could feel her face turning red at the exchange between the two of them. This was not a conversation she was accustomed to having with senior officers. *God, Shveta, you are so bold*, she thought. "Oh, Shveta, I'm sure the Lieutenant Commander doesn't mean any harm. He's just another guy who isn't used to having women on the base. So, maybe we should cut him a little slack?" Katy tried to be as nonchalant and cocky as Shveta, but even to her ears it sounded lame.

"Katy, I'm telling you, watch out for this one," Shveta said with a smile. But, her eyes told Katy she was serious.

"Well, ladies, what's it going to be? Can I get you something or not?"

"I actually need to leave. I'm on duty roster tonight," Shveta said. "Katy, are you coming?"

Katy looked at Shveta knowing she should go as well but, instead, decided against it. "No, Shveta, I'm going to let the Lieutenant Commander buy me a cold Diet Coke. You go on. I promise I'll be OK," she said as she waved Shveta on. "I'll catch up with you in the morning."

"OK," Shveta said, frowning, very obviously displeased with Katy's decision. "I'll check on you tomorrow." She threw Jack a threatening look.

"I promise not a hair on her pretty little head will be harmed," Jack said, laughing.

Katy watched Shveta leave and then turned to Jack as he paid for her Coke.

"Do you want a little something mixed in this, Katy?" he asked as he pulled a flask from his shirt pocket.

Caught off guard by his use of her first name, she said, "Lieutenant Commander, do you think it's OK to call me Katy? What if someone hears you?" She looked around the cafe to see if anyone had actually heard him.

"I can call you Second Lieutenant if you want, but it seems much easier to have a conversation if I just call you Katy and you call me Jack. Don't you think?"

"Umm . . . yes, I suppose you're right. I guess I'm just not used to the more relaxed protocol here on the base. Remember, I'm coming directly from the Fort Bragg chain of command and whatnot. I'm sorry if I'm a little stiff . . . I'll get used to things, I'm sure," Katy said apologetically, feeling embarrassed by her adherence to decorum.

"Hey, don't worry about it. You'll figure it out. I've been watching you, and I can see how smart and adaptable you are. Besides, a little of this," he waved the flask in front of her, "can get rid of any stiffness. How did such a pretty face get so smart, anyway?"

"Oh, now you are just being outright flirtatious," Katy said, calling him out on his comment. "And no, I don't want any liquor." *Is this guy for real?* she thought. "How many women have you used that line on?"

"No one who has ever called me on it," he said, smiling at her. "Katy, in all seriousness, I find myself very attracted to you, and you know . . . out here in this godforsaken country . . . I just thought maybe we could get to know each other a little better," he said, moving his barstool closer to hers. "I promise if you tell me to go away, I will, but I will go with a broken heart." He clutched his heart. "Katy don't break my heart," he said with big, blue, puppy-dog eyes and a smile that could melt ice. "Just promise you will give me a chance."

Katy shook her head at his over-the-top demonstration, then gave him a sideways glance. "I suspect I'm going to be sorry I said this, but . . . what the hell? Who's it going to hurt?" she said, with one eyebrow raised and a slight edge of skepticism in her voice.

Laughing out loud, Jack said, "Well, I'm not sure that's exactly the response I wanted, but I'm going to take that as a yes."

"OK, Jack," she laughed with him. "Here's to getting to know each other." They clinked their plastic cups together. "Does it ever cool off here?" she asked, wiping the sweat from her face with a paper napkin.

"No, unfortunately for now, this is it. Makes you yearn for the fall and winter days of New England, doesn't it?"

"Hmm . . . that does sound wonderful. I once took a trip to Plattsburgh, New York, during late September. It was beautiful. The colors of fall, the crispness of the air. It was exhilarating. I was so energized there. I'll never forget that visit."

"Ah, Katy, you have to see the Intercoastal Waterway out of Maryland. Water as far as the eye can see, with quaint little houses along the shoreline. I sailed it one year, all the way from Florida up the East Coast. It was an incredible trip."

Their conversation once again took on an ease that was new for Katy. During high school she had not had time for boys, what with her athletic activities and work. In college, she dated occasionally, but, once she became involved in ROTC, she just didn't have time for relationships. Besides, once she joined the Army, most of the men in her life were superior officers she thought of as father figures or troops who were her subordinates. Romantic nuances were new ground for her, and she felt unsure of herself.

As promised, Jack got her back to her quarters safely and, with a small kiss on her cheek, bid her goodnight. Feeling strangely disconcerted but decidedly good, Katy readied herself for sleep.

CHAPTER IV

Loving someone deeply gives you courage.

—LAO TZU

KANDAHAR, AFGHANISTAN
MAY 2012

Base life continued in full swing, and missions into the field started to feel more comfortable. Shveta took more of a back seat as Katy developed her skills, and the entire team was starting to gel. The debriefings the team went through after each mission were conducted by a senior officer as well as the base psychologist. At first, Katy thought these were a waste of everyone's time. But, over time, she saw the unit's cohesion become stronger as they shared not only what happened during each mission but also their feelings about what happened. Jack was on most of the missions with her as Flight Surgeon for the MEDEVAC team. Katy noticed that, while he spoke up in the debriefings, he never really shared his feelings about the missions. In fact, when the group started talking about feelings, he would get up and leave.

One night, about five months into her tour, Katy was coming off a night-duty shift and saw the mission helicopters landing. There were ambulances speeding toward the landing pod. She ran over to the perimeter to see if she could help and find out what happened. As the dust settled, she saw a stretcher being lifted from the helicopter's bay. It was Jack.

She ducked under the perimeter and ran over to the stretcher.

"Jack, what happened? Are you all right?" she asked, grabbing his hand. He was sitting upright on the stretcher, and she could see he was alert, awake, and smiling.

"Well, well, Katy girl, what are you doing here? I'm fine, no worries, just a little graze to the arm." Katy thought he was acting strange.

"Oh my God, Jack, what happened?" she asked as the medics pushed the gurney toward the ambulance.

"Oh, it was just bullshit! The place was supposed to be secure, and out of nowhere a sniper starts picking off the boys in the middle of the village square. Pissed me off to no end! So, I jumped out of the bird, picked up an M4, and starting shooting.

I wasn't going to let the boys lay there on the ground to be captured later."

"Yeah, Katy, but he's not telling you the part where I had to physically force the M4 from his hands and drag his ass back to the helicopter, so we could leave," Skip, the helicopter pilot, interjected as he walked up to the stretcher. Katy had flown several missions with Skip and knew he was a very competent pilot. "I came this close to cold-cocking this stupid bastard. He almost got us all killed! Thankfully someone else shot him, and that put an end to his one-man show!"

Katy couldn't tell if he was really angry or if it was just the adrenaline in his voice.

"Oh, Skip, I'm just glad to see you guys back. It must have been terrible."

"Katy, Katy, this was an easy run," Jack said, still filled with bravado.

Skip just shook his head. "Thanks, Katy, I'll catch you later," he said and walked away.

"Oh, I guarantee I'm going to hear about this one," Jack said, looking at Katy. "Really, it was nothing. In my opinion, the mission was screwed up from the beginning, and all I did was make sure no one was left behind. Don't worry about me, Katy girl, I'm going to be just fine."

Katy helped the medics fold the stretcher wheels up so that it would fit into the ambulance and watched as they drove away. *My God, Jack, what were you doing?* she wondered.

—

The next morning found Katy sitting in the cafeteria, which was alive with the buzz of last night's near escape. She was eating powdered scrambled eggs that were wet and soggy. They tasted horrible. She usually didn't eat cafeteria eggs, but she was hungry this morning and knew she probably wouldn't eat again until late evening. Shveta and a couple of other members of her team were sitting with her when Jack strolled up, his arm in a sling.

"Ladies, gentlemen," he offered as he sat down next to Katy.

"Hey, Jack, how are you feeling?" Katy asked.

"Oh, don't worry about that crazy bastard, Katy. This isn't the first time he's been shot for doing stupid shit," one of the guys at the table said. "This is a minor injury compared to the last time."

Katy shot a look at Jack. "The last time?"

"Oh, it was no big deal. Everyone went a little crazy because I had blood spurting from my leg, but—"

"Atten-shun!" was shouted from a corner in the cafeteria as the base commander walked in.

Looking around the room, he walked over to the table where Katy and the rest of the group were standing at attention.

"Lieutenant Commander Foster, you are to report to my office at 0800 sharp! Is that clear?"

"Yes sir, 0800. I'll be there, sir," Jack replied.

The commander turned. As he exited, he yelled, "At ease," and the buzz and activity in the cafeteria picked up where it had left off.

"Jack, what's going on?" Katy asked.

"Nothing to worry about, Katy. The old man is just going to ream my ass for what happened last night. Not like I haven't been reamed out before."

"Jack, this is serious. He's not someone to fool with."

"Katy, he will have his say, but there are no other Flight Surgeons who do what I do. So, he'll yell, I'll say mea culpa, and that will be that. Listen, I gotta go. Just wanted to say hi." Looking up at everyone at the table, he said, "I'll see you all later," and walked out of the cafeteria.

As he left, Katy noticed that several men stopped him to pat him on the shoulder or shake his hand.

"Shveta, what gives with Jack? It seems like everyone here thinks he's something special."

"Not as special as Jack thinks he is," Shveta said sarcastically.

"Shveta! Really, he's done some good work here. Why don't you like him?"

"I can't put my finger on it, but you Americans would say 'My spidey sensors are prickling' whenever I talk to that guy."

Katy laughed at her awkward attempt at an Americanism. "Oh, Shveta, no one makes me laugh like you do. I gotta go. I'm due for a briefing, and then I'm supposed to go out on a convoy with the boys. I'll see you later." Getting up from the table, she leaned over and gave Shveta a hug. "You're the best," she said and waved goodbye.

As she walked over to the briefing hut, Katy brushed off Shveta's concerns. *He's a good guy, just looking out for his men. When you think about it, he is pretty special. I can see why people love him. He's always the first to volunteer for a mission or to jump out and risk his neck for his men.* Her thoughts were accompanied by a warm nurturing feeling that was unfamiliar to her.

About a week later, while returning from late-night watch duty, Katy saw Jack sitting by himself on the stoop of his quarters with a half-empty bottle of liquor in his hands. *I wonder what's going on,* she thought. She hesitated in the shadows of his quarters as she listened to the haunting song playing on his iPhone,

I reach for him in the morning and he's not there
And I remember we're parted by sea and air
As I dress and put on my make-up and get ready to leave

Letters of Forgiveness

The kids and I miss you, at breakfast and we grieve
The kids ask me "Mommy, how long will Daddy be gone?"
What do I tell them, that battle lines have been drawn.
Do I tell them, "Be proud of Daddy for fighting off this attack."
Or do I tell them I am scared, worried you won't come back?
Lord, where is my husband? Is he safe with you today?
All our hearts are aching; please hear the prayer I pray.
Dear God, be with him and keep him safe and warm.
Help us all to weather this separation storm.
God, return him to me. I know he misses us too.
In all that sand and hatred, he must be feeling so blue.
I pray that soon he returns to our little family affair.
When I reach for him in the morning, he'll be there.

Slowly coming out of the shadows, she walked toward him. "Wow, what a bittersweet song. Jack . . . is everything alright? Are you OK? How's the arm doing?" He had stopped wearing the sling a couple of days ago.

Jack looked up at her from his seated position. "Katy, Katy, Katy, where have you been all my life?" he said, his speech slurred.

"What?"

"Katy, sit down." He reached up and pulled her arm hard enough to force her to sit next to him on the stoop.

"Jack, I think you've had a little too much to drink," she said as she reached for the bottle in his hand. He immediately moved it out of her reach. She wasn't sure what she was supposed to do. "Maybe I can help you into your quarters or get you some coffee? You're not on call tonight, are you?"

"No, I'm not on fucking call, and I don't want coffee," he growled. "Or maybe I do want coffee. I can mix this hooch I have in it. Or maybe I'll just drink it straight up. Katy, what do you know about having babies?" he asked, waving his arm and the bottle of liquor around wildly.

"I beg your pardon?" she replied, pulling away from him.

"Do you have any children, Second Lieutenant?" he asked, again grabbing her arm to hold her next to him.

"No sir, I'm not married."

"Oh . . . so you think you have to be married to have children?" Jack said mockingly. Shaking his index finger at her and slurring heavily, he said, "Let me tell you something . . . it isn't a requirement. You just need—"

Katy cut him off. "That's not what I meant, and you know it." She grabbed his accusatory finger.

"Katy, Katy, Katy," he said as he put his arm around her shoulders and pulled her close to his side. "You would never—"

"Umm . . . Jack, this is probably not a good idea right here," she replied. However, she found his touch intoxicating even if he did reek of alcohol.

At that moment, he leaned into her and kissed her hard on the mouth. "You're right," he said. He quickly stood, picked her up in his arms, and took her into his quarters. Katy squealed in protest but did not fight him.

Once inside his quarters, the developing chemistry between them coupled with the stress of their environment lit a passion that rivaled the fire of the gods.

—

After that evening, there were very few days where they didn't spend time in each other's arms. They laughed, made plans about going home, and shared their lives on base with each other. Both of them loved the water and laughed themselves silly as they thought of ways to devise a sailboat that could traverse Afghanistan's rough desert terrain and mountainous plateaus. They even built a toy sailboat out of popsicle sticks together.

Katy did not tell Shveta about the affair. She was sure Shveta would not approve, and she did not want to risk their friendship or working relationship over it. It was hard to keep secret because Katy wanted to shout it from the mountaintops, but she knew discretion was her best bet. Despite her surroundings, the daily threat to life, and the interminable heat, Katy was happy. When the moon rose over the eastern hills and the stars were out in full, Katy thought Afghanistan was the most romantic place in the world.

Dimitri & Elena

CHAPTER V

Do not go gentle into that good night but rage,
rage against the dying of the light.

—DYLAN THOMAS

WASHINGTON, DC
JUNE 2012

Dimitri was sleeping when they found him in the alley, wrapped up in a tattered sleeping bag under a cardboard box. He wore an old, ill-fitting, black wool coat. It made him appear very small though he was a tall, lanky man. The place reeked of garbage and human stench but was home for a number of people. Many of them slept near liquor bottles. Others were only half asleep, rocking themselves back and forth, trying to dispel imaginary demons. This was the alley where the disenfranchised and homeless congregated nightly. They were the people of the night, some mentally ill, others destitute, or simply living off the grid. Dimitri Demidova had been led here by a nameless wretch who offered to share her vodka with him. But, Dimitri was not homeless—he was just lost.

Two days ago, he had wandered away from Harbor Place in the Village, a skilled nursing home and rehabilitation facility in Washington, D.C. The facility was his new home, and he was not happy there. The many rules and rigid structure were too much for an eighty-four-year-old man who had fled the Soviet Union during the Cold War. But, he was unable to live alone. About six months ago, his progressing dementia led him to accidentally cause a fire in his apartment, and that was the last straw for his daughter, Elena. She placed him in the facility less than three days after the fire. It happened so quickly that he had no time to protest. But, ever since the move, he had been a flight risk and, once again, he had managed to escape.

Facility staff had been looking for him for the last two days. Law enforcement was also on alert. A silver alert was issued, and finally someone called in about an elderly man wearing a long black coat staggering down an alleyway on Fifth Street. Staff found him lying on the ground with an empty bottle of vodka, drunk and not easily aroused.

"Dimitri," the aide said as he shook him. "Come on, man. Get up, and let's go home."

Dimitri opened one eye to look at him but did not recognize him. He turned away to go back to sleep.

"Come on, old man. It's time to go. You've had enough freedom for a while. We've been looking for you for two days now," the aide said in exasperation.

The words and tone had a familiar threat to them, and Dimitri started to struggle.

"Oh shit! Dave, we're going to need restraints. Get them out of the van, will you?"

Dimitri struggled, but he did not have the strength to put up much of a fight. He was old, intoxicated, and had not eaten in two days.

The two aides managed to restrain him and got him into the van without anyone getting hurt. The ride back was short, and Anna, his nurse, was waiting for him. She removed his restraints and took his arm to lead him to his room.

"*Devi,* [1] Dimitri, let's get you cleaned up. Woo-boy, do you stink. What have you been up to? Are you hungry?" Anna asked.

"*Da, ya goladen,*" [2] he replied in his native tongue, forgetting that her Russian was very limited.

It didn't matter. Anna walked him to his room, where she undressed him and put him in the shower to scrub him down.

---

1   "Come on."
2   "Yes, I'm hungry."

"Now that's a lot better!" she said, smiling as she helped him into his pajamas. It was late, but Anna had a soft spot for Dimitri. Knowing he had probably not eaten in a couple of days, she had chicken soup and a turkey sandwich waiting for him. Exchanging very few words, she sat him down and spoon fed him the soup. Confused and speaking only in Russian, Dimitri slowly seemed to calm down as Anna fed him and gently tried to soothe his confused mind.

"Oh, Dimitri, I know you must have had an interesting life. Maybe one day you will tell this tired old nurse something interesting," she said, smiling at him, speaking softly as she fed him the last of the soup. After he finished eating, she got him into bed and sat with him until he fell asleep. Afterward, she called his daughter to let her know they had found him . . . again.

The next day, he was sitting in the Harbor Place great room gazing out the window when he heard her.

"Papa! What have you done?"

Her voice snapped him out of the black hole he was in.

"Papa, thank God you are safe! Where did you go this time? Why do you keep doing this? What is wrong with you, are you being mistreated? Are they not feeding you? Maybe you don't like your room? What am I supposed to do, Papa? I cannot be here every day with you. I have my life! This is the life *you* brought me to. Now you are punishing me by scaring me to death! What . . . *pochemu*?"[3] she admonished him.

In his softest voice reserved just for her, his little girl, he said, "*Moy ziechick.*"[4]

"No, Papa, *nyet*! You cannot pour sugar on your words this time! I am too angry with you! I am at my wit's end and, so are the people here. They tell me if you leave again, they will send you away from here! Is that what you want? Do you really want to live on the streets with the drunks and those people who cannot think straight anymore?"

He looked up at her.

"Yes, they told me where they found you. What about Sasha and Tasha? You are a *dedushka*![5] What do I tell them if you are living on the streets—"

"My Elena, you worry so about your Papa. Why? Do you not remember that I have survived worse?" He spoke with such clarity that she stopped talking. "Do you not remember the nights when I held you so close to me, hidden away in the coal train? What did I tell you then?" His voice softened. "I told you that I would always be there for you in the darkest of night. Do you remember?"

---

3   "What . . . why?""

4   "My little bunny."

5   "You are a grandfather!"

She felt tears welling up in her eyes as she looked at this man who had brought her to the United States from Communist Russia. How could she forget that train? How could she ever forget the acrid smell of diesel fuel and black coal dust choking her, causing her to vomit over and over again? At the time, she had not known where they were going. She remembered being carried on his back while he climbed a ladder up to the top of a coal car and, then, sitting in coal for days with no food. She remembered how frightened she'd been when he was so cold one night, she could not get him to speak to her. But, most of all, what she remembered, and had never really forgiven him of, was leaving her mother behind. She'd been ten years old when they fled Russia.

Eventually, they made it to Washington, D.C. But, it was a place where she had no connections and no understanding of the language. Hating him through most of her tween years, she'd worked at making him miserable. It was not right that he had left her mother and taken her away. Growing up, her hair was messy, her clothes were mismatched, and the other kids constantly made fun of her accent.

In Russia, they were somebody, especially her mother, who was a prima ballerina with the Bolshoi Ballet. They could have stayed and lived a grand life with the ballet. Elena had been training with her mother and had hopes of becoming a prima ballerina herself one day.

Dimitri was a writer. Elena recalled multiple screaming matches between her father and her mother over his writing. Her mother had said that one day his writing was going to get them all killed. Elena had been seven or eight years old at the time. She had not understood why the concepts of freedom, justice, and human rights were so important to him. All she knew was that she'd been forbidden to talk about such things among her friends. Her mother had warned her that there were "ears everywhere," and she should limit her conversations to schoolwork, dancing, and other things that young girls usually spoke about.

Home life had been very confusing. One minute, she'd be with her mother backstage at a theater, talking with the greats of ballet and the next, with her father, where politics was the only topic of conversation. Elena hated politics.

Her mother, the great Galina, had insisted Elena learn to dance. When Elena complained about the endless hours of practice, her mother would remind her, "Elena, this will ensure you never have to live like a commoner. The politburo is always looking for the next great dancer. It will be you, Elena, but only if you practice. Now, Elena, *devi*. Again, one and two and three . . . "

So, Elena had learned to dance from the very best in Russia, Nina Ananiashvili, Nikolai Fadeyechev, and Alexander Godunov, to name a few. Despite her complaints, she'd loved it.

She'd actually had her first crush on one young man who could leap higher than she had ever seen. He was beautiful when he danced, and all of Russia was in love with him. They called him Misha, and he was Elena's first love. But, then he ran away. Her father said it was the government's fault that he ran away. For a while she fantasized that he would return to Russia to dance with her, but Mikhail Baryshnikov would never return to Russia.

Her father tried to teach her, too, about ideas from another world she did not understand and had no interest in. His writing was the source of so much worry in her home that she refused to read any of it. She also stubbornly refused to learn English from him. She remembered reading about the dissident poet Anna Akhmatova and how her poetry had caused her such great sorrow. She did not want to live a life like Anna's.

So, she followed closely in her mother's footsteps and focused on her dancing. She became the Bolshoi's young sweetheart, and, at the age of ten, she danced the part of Clara in *The Nutcracker*. It was the happiest moment in her young life. It was a magnificent coup for such a young girl, and she knew it. Her future career had been solidified on that day. The accolades she received immediately after the show were outstanding, and even the mayor stopped to say hello and congratulate her. She could still hear the roar of the audience as she took her final bow.

On the night of her final performance, Dimitri had come to take her home. It was the typical routine after one of her mother's performances. The cast was joyous. Elena was walking on clouds, and Galina was showing her off to everyone.

"Mr. Mayor, please, I would like to introduce you to my daughter," Galina said.

"Oh, so this is your tiny dancer, Galina. She moves like you. You were very good up there, young lady," he said.

"*Spaciba*,"[6] Elena replied, curtsying as she had been taught to do.

"Galina!" someone shouted from the far left of the stage. "I want to meet your young protégé."

Galina took Elena's hand, and they were off to meet another visitor. Afterward, her mother took her back to her dressing room and wrapped her in her fur coat, kissed her over and over again, and sent her out the theater door with her father. Elena felt something wasn't right but said nothing. The cold and bitter Russian night bit into Elena's cheeks, but her mother's coat was warm. She felt so grown-up wearing it. Elena thought her

---

6   "Thank you."

mother had wrapped her in the coat as a reward for dancing well. She was unaware of the journey she was about to take.

—

After arriving in the United States, the government gave Dimitri a job as a paid consultant in Russian affairs. His knowledge of Russia and his writing skills were welcomed and well-received in the Foreign Affairs Bureau. Elena wasn't exactly sure what he did, but she felt like he was telling stories about her beloved Russia that she didn't think should be told, stories about gulags and false imprisonment, corruption in the government, and how the government had betrayed its people.

They made their home in a small apartment in Washington, D.C. She was enrolled in fourth grade immediately, and her first year of school was a complete nightmare. How she wished she had learned some English when her father had tried to teach her! But, she would never admit that to him. In those days, she had no friends and cried almost every day after school. It was her increasing despondency that led Dimitri to enroll her at a ballroom dance studio.

At the studio, Elena found kindred spirits in the other dancers. Most of the teachers were Russian and could communicate with her easily. It was such a relief to be able to finally talk to someone, but they also insisted she learn English. Her teachers were fascinated by the tiny girl with the auburn hair and intense green eyes. Her energy and initial insolence was challenging yet amusing to them, and they immediately took her under their collective wings. She struggled at first, but, with her new family encouraging her, English became easier. By the end of fifth grade, she was speaking fluently.

However, her ballet training did not serve her well in ballroom dancing, and she had to work hard to learn how to roll her feet from heel to toe. But, her gorgeous extensions and lines did not go unnoticed. She quickly became the darling of the studio. At sixteen, she was introduced to Andrei Gorchenko, another young Russian dancer who had grown up in a ballroom studio. Andrei was sandy-haired with green eyes that seemed very deep when she looked into them. He had an angular jaw and dimples that made him quite handsome. At five feet, eleven inches tall, he was quiet and introspective, but there was no denying the emotion he displayed when he danced. Both talented as well as smart, Lena and Andrei hit it off immediately. She finally had a best friend. They won competition after competition and were constantly sought out for performances. Everyone thought she and Andrei would make the perfect couple and would marry someday, but it wasn't like that between them. They were just good friends. In fact, when the owners of the studio put it up for sale, it was Andrei who approached Lena about buying the studio together. It was an easy sell, and when Elena was twenty-six years old, she and Andrei became business partners.

—

Over time, Lena's relationship with her father softened. Whether she liked it or not, he was her responsibility now and she would not, could not, dismiss him. Even so, she was unable to let go of the underlying anger and resentment she held against her father for leaving her mother behind in Russia. It was a chasm that separated them in spirit. Slowly returning back to the present after flashing through the memories of how she and her father had arrived here, she looked at closely at her father.

"Papa, please promise me. No more," she pleaded with Dimitri. "Sasha and Tasha want their *Dedushka* to stay healthy for them."

"What about you, Lena? What do you want?" Dimitri asked her.

"Peace, Papa, just a little peace," she said as she leaned over to kiss him goodbye. "Promise me, Papa, please, no more escapes."

Dimitri just smiled as she walked away. Memories of his own mother and father flooded his thoughts.

CHAPTER VI

For a country to have a great writer is like having
a second government. That is why no regime has
ever loved great writers, only minor ones.

—ALEKSANDR SOLZHENITSYN

OUTSIDE MOSCOW, RUSSIA
1929-1943

Dimitri Victorvich Demidova was the only son of Russian
farmer Victor Ivanovich Demidova. He was born July 4, 1929,
one year after Stalin took power from Lenin, just outside of
Moscow, the great city in Russia. Dimitri lived with his mother,
a pretty, blue-eyed Siberian blonde, and his father, a muscular
and handsome man with dark black eyes, black hair, and a beard.
Dimitri looked much like his father.

Victor was a working farmer, one of the few who still owned
the land he worked. At the age of five, Dimitri learned to carry
water up from the stream to the garden and to load baskets of

produce collected from the yearly harvests. Side by side, every year, Dimitri and his father brought the cold, frozen ground of Mother Russia to life. Working alongside his father, Dimitri grew to love and respect him dearly. While they worked the land together, his father shared stories about his life.

Dimitri's father would tell him about the great revolution and World War I. "War is never an answer, my son," he said repeatedly while they worked. "It brings only misery and robs young men of their dignity and their minds."

Victor told Dimitri stories about the suffering he had witnessed during the Revolution and the war. Stories of men who had toes fall off from frostbite as they tramped through the bitterly cold snow with nothing more than rags on their feet. How dysentery, typhus, trench foot, and the bitter cold ran through legions of men. How he walked by frozen corpses, many with their hands raised as if they made one last effort to summon help, and about men who sat around campfires pulling handfuls of lice from their armpits, beards, and groins. "That was the real war, Dimitri," he would say, "men trying to exist in inhumane conditions while killing their brothers. Trying to remain sane after what they saw and did. It is impossible."

Dimitri knew the war had left his father with a deep, emotional scar.

Victor also always demanded that Dimitri put his family responsibilities first. "Dema, you must always do what is best for your family," his father would say. "It is your job to protect them and provide for them. You must be ever vigilant to their needs. When the days come where you have nothing, if you are wise, you will still always have family."

His mother was a poet. She had met Victor after he returned from the war. It was her kindness and poetry that eventually brought Victor back to life. She loved Russia and wrote about the beauty of the country and its working-class people. Dimitri had a favorite poem that she would recite each night at bedtime as she tucked him in.

The bosom of mother Russia
Remains firm for all her children
Do not cry for her, ye men of little faith.
She will always be there for you.
Eat her berries and drink her water.
She provides these for your life.
Walk her mountains, warm yourself in her sun.
And when the stars come out
Lay down your sleepy heads
And she will cradle you into the morn.

Life was hard for his family, but they were together. And, they had food to eat, unlike so many other families suffering from the great famine. Victor made sure they shared with their neighbors whenever possible. Dimitri's father showed him how to plow the earth and seed the land, how to raise hens for their eggs and, later, for their meat. His mother insisted he also attend school.

The Great Russian Revolution of 1917 had led to a particular emphasis on literacy. Schools were built, and laws were passed to ensure children went to school and learned to read and write. The Bolsheviks' focus was on developing the child's mind and personality. The philosophy was that once a child was old enough, they would naturally select topics they were proficient in. For Dimitri, those topics were reading and writing. Even at a young age, he could never get enough to read. He read the works of Tolstoy, Gogol, Chekov, and Gorky and studied social and economic theories as well as philosophy. By the time he was ready for high school, he was reading and writing at a university level.

At night, by candlelight, visitors came to his home, people whom his father and mother sat with while they whispered secrets and stories. Dimitri settled on the floor behind the big green armchair in the living room, where his father always sat wrapped in a homemade quilt and listened to them talk. He did not know it at the time, but the guests were infamous in Russia. Anna Akhmatova, Marina Tsvetaeva, and Vasily Grossman were a few of the numerous visitors. Laughing, crying, and drinking vodka, the group shared stories of the Revolution and the war. They discussed the ongoing famine that followed, and they lamented the loss of their loved ones. Always whispering amongst themselves as if someone were in the home listening, Dimitri heard them discuss Stalin and the terror and shame he had brought to Russia. How Stalin's policy of collectivization was taking away the private farmer's dignity and stealing his land. They branded Stalin a thief, a liar, and a traitor to the Revolution. But, they all understood one thing. Stalin was ruthless, and he was feared by all. Stories of Stalin's betrayal to Mother Russia filled Dimitri's head, and by the time he was twelve, Dimitri had found his own voice of dissent. His mother and father were proud of him, but they feared for him and warned him that this path was a dangerous one. His mother hid his writings in a secret compartment in her bureau drawer.

One night, when Dimitri was fourteen, there was a knock on the door. Dimitri opened it and instantly froze. There stood four members of the dreaded NKVD.[7] The NKVD were infamous for their brutality and for arresting anyone who disagreed with Stalin. Deportation of political prisoners, landowners,

---

7   *Narodnyy Komissariat Vnutrennikh Del.* The People's Commissariat for Internal Affairs.

political dissidents, families, and other innocents to forced labor camps or gulags was a heinous reality to the locals. Stalin had empowered the NKVD to singlehandedly investigate, arrest, interrogate, prosecute, try, and render a guilty verdict in the span of a few hours. People went missing daily, never to be heard from again. These were Stalin's enforcers, the predecessors of the KGB secret police. Ruthless, unregulated, corrupt, and merciless, their sole purpose was to eliminate anyone deemed a threat to the politburo or Stalin himself. During Stalin's regime, over 3 million people went missing. Stalin's prisoners were a cheap labor force for the politburo, and he used them to build infrastructure and mine the mounts of Russia until they dropped dead.

It was May when that fateful knock on the door occurred. The ground was finally thawing, and Dimitri and his father had laid sunflower and corn seeds in the farm's back lot. The two cows were finally grazing outside again, and milk was plentiful. Dimitri loved the smell of the soft black earth coming alive again. Tantalizing Dimitri with its promise of new growth and a productive summer, it was his favorite time of year. He looked forward to the work he and his father would do.

"*Gde Victor Ivanovich?*"[8] demanded the officer, entering the home with his dirty black jackboots stomping mud on the floor.

---

8   "Where is Victor Ivanovich?"

"*Ya ne znayu,*"[9] Dimitri lied, his small frame trembling at the sight of the tall, threatening officer standing in front of him.

Suddenly, the officer slammed Dimitri up against the wall and held him there while the other two pulled the house apart looking for anything that might be considered incriminating.

"*Chto vy ishchete?*"[10] Dimitri yelled. He felt the harsh wood of the officer's baton against his skull. What happened afterward remained unclear, as the blow knocked him to the ground and left him severely dazed. Dimitri lay there, bleeding and unable to move. He remembered hearing his mother scream in horror as he was struck (she must have come in through the back door), and, shortly thereafter, he thought he heard gunshots. But, the rest was a memory he would never recover. When he woke, his head was in his father's lap, and they were in a cattle car traveling the rails of Russia with another fifty or so people.

Victor tenderly helped his son sit up. Dimitri saw his father was weeping, and he knew something terrible had happened.

"Papa, what happened?"

"Dema . . . " he choked on the words. "My son, my son," was all he could say as he held Dimitri close to his chest and wept.

"Papa, *gde Mamulia?*"[11]

---

9   "I don't know.

10   "What are you looking for?"

11   "Where is Momma?"

Through his shock and tears, Victor told his son, "Momma is dead, they shot her because she wanted to keep them away from the bureau drawer. Why didn't she just let . . . ? Why did they have to shoot her? Dema, I would have given my life for her . . . why did they shoot her?" he asked over and over again as he choked back his sobs.

It took a few minutes for Dimitri to understand, but the more it sank in, the greater his rage grew. "Papa, where are we going?" he asked in a whisper.

"To the Lubyanka in Moscow," Victor said flatly.

"We have to escape, Papa, now! We can jump from this train and be gone. They won't even notice. How will they tell? Look at us, crammed onto this train as if we were cows being taken to slaughter."

"We are," Victor replied.

"Papa, now! We must get out of here."

Victor looked over at the railcar's huge sliding doors, and then Dimitri noticed the two guards armed with machine guns.

"Papa, what are we going to do?" Dimitri asked in a frightened whisper.

"Survive," was Victor's simple response.

Finally, the train slowed, and the guards demanded they get off. Those who were infirm or disabled were pushed, shoved, or thrown from the train. Their fellow captives tried to help them but painfully received the short end of their jailer's baton for interfering. It was a short walk from the train station. As Dimitri and Victor turned the corner, the infamous Lubyanka loomed up ahead.

The Lubyanka was a large building with a faded yellow brick facade. It had been designed by Alexander V. Ivanov in 1897 and served as headquarters for the NKVD. In its basement, innocent victims of Stalin's purges were imprisoned. Most of those who entered under armed guard were never heard from again.

Their arrival at the Lubyanka was mostly theatrics. There was a short hearing without either Dimitri or his father present. They were convicted of conspiracy against the government and for this they received a "tenner," or ten-year sentence of hard labor in a gulag. In that moment, Dimitri's world plunged over the precipice from freedom into the hell of imprisonment.

After the "trial," his father was taken away and interrogated over several days. Each time he returned bloodied and barely conscious. Dema did what he could for him, but, without access to running water or even a toilet, there was very little he could do to help. "Papa, what do they want from you?"

"Blood," was his vague reply.

Dimitri was sure that his father was being punished because of his writings. "Papa, I wrote those papers that Momma hid. It should be me, not you."

Through swollen, black-and-blue eyes, Victor looked sternly at Dimitri and said, "Dimitri, they did not find your writings when they searched the house. Your mother was much too clever for them. But *never* speak of those papers again!" His tone softened. "My son, you will go on. It is your destiny to write about freedom for our people. Do this for your mother. She would be proud." Dimitri saw the tears in his father's eyes. "She gave her life for us, Dema. Don't ever forget that debt. You will one day get out of here," Victor said as he lay limp in Dimitri's arms.

In the dim light, Dimitri could see that his father's eyes were almost swollen shut, his teeth were broken, and his left arm was flaccid. That night, Dimitri swore that one day he would avenge his family. In the meantime, all he could do was weep for his father who was as limp as a puppet lying in his lap.

On day four, they were boarded into a cattle car that would take them and approximately one hundred other prisoners to their final destination. Men, women, children, the mentally ill, and the disabled—although they were usually just shot— were all crammed together into the car. There were no toilets, only buckets or holes in the floorboards, and the stench was horrific. Children were sick to their stomachs from lack of food and the train's momentum. The elderly could not contain their bowels or bladders and were covered in urine and feces.

Women tried to remain modest, but, unless there was someone to shield them as they relieved themselves, they just had to bear the embarrassment. It didn't take long for dysentery to set in, and, by the tenth day, bodies were being thrown out of the rattling car. The elderly were not up to the rigors of dehydration, dysentery, and the bone-chilling cold. There was barely any food and water, and days would go by without either. When there was something to eat, it was usually a cold liquid broth with some rice filled with maggots and other creatures. Dimitri bribed the guards with a few smuggled cigarettes he snuck out of Lubyanka to get them extra rations, but it wasn't much. He gave what he could get to his father. Victor's injuries were severe, and Dimitri worried he might die.

The nights grew colder as they traveled over the next two weeks. Dimitri could tell they were headed north by the change in the climate. Without proper clothing and protection from the cold, he feared his father would not survive it. Many of the elderly continued to die, and their unidentified bodies were thrown from the train to lie frozen in the desolate north, unburied and unmourned. One night, as the guards rounded up bodies to throw from the train, Dimitri took the clothes off one of the dead. Before anyone could see what he had done, he threw the body from the train. Praying for forgiveness, he went back to his father and put the extra ragged clothing on him. Victor did not speak. He just looked at his son with lifeless eyes.

After what seemed like an eternity, the train finally stopped. When the doors of the railcar opened, it was worse than Dimitri had imagined. They were in Vanino, the first stop to Kolyma.

CHAPTER VII

Unlimited power in the hands of limited
people always leads to cruelty.

—ALEKSANDR SOLZHENITSYN

EASTERN SIBERIA
1943-1953

Kolyma is surrounded by the East Siberian Sea and the Arctic Ocean in the north and the Sea of Okhotsk to the south. Located in the far northeast corner of Siberia, it is a cold and inhospitable place. The region gets its name from the Kolyma River and mountain range. Because of its location within the Arctic Circle, winters in Kolyma last up to six months with permafrost and tundra covering a large part of the region. Winter temperatures range from -40 to -2 degrees Fahrenheit, and average summer temperatures reach only 60 degrees. In the late 1920s, coal and other precious commodities were discovered in the Kolyma Mountains.

Stalin's projects needed considerable financial backing, and the gold and other commodities found within Kolyma's harsh terrain were exactly what he needed to fund his plans. The inhospitable climate, isolated location, and sparse populace made it a perfect place to establish forced labor camps. Tens of thousands died en route to the area, and those who lived there said even the roads were built with the bodies of the dead. Aleksandr Solzhenitsyn described Kolyma as the "pole of cold and cruelty."

Initial efforts to develop the region started with Magadan. Located in the harbor of the Sea of Okhotsk, Magadan was the first entryway into Kolyma. Using the Trans-Siberian Railway, prisoners were herded onto train cars like cattle and transported to Nakhodka or Vanino. If they survived the brutal rail ride, they were then crammed into slave ships that crossed the Sea of Okhotsk to Magadan. The constant danger of getting caught in the Arctic ice made the trip particularly challenging. Thousands more died while crossing due to starvation and the unrelenting, vicious cold.

Using Magadan as a home base, expeditions explored the interior of Kolyma. Exploration required roads. In the harshest of conditions, with little food or clothing, prisoners were forced to build the interior roads. The Kolyma Highway became known as the Road of Bones, and, eventually, eighty different gulags were established in the region.

But there was no end to Stalin's cruelty, and, in 1937, at the height of the Purges, he issued an order to intensify the hardships that prisoners endured. Camp commander Naftaly Frenkel famously said, as he established the new mandate, "We have to squeeze everything out of a prisoner in the first three months—after that we don't need him anymore." In other words, prisoners fell quickly, victims of the fourteen-hour workday, minimal food, and precious little clothing to protect them from the weather. Inmates labeled their fellow prisoners as *dokhodyagi*[12] as they became weak and sick. Malnutrition, dysentery, typhus, and other communicable diseases ravaged their bodies. Kolyma was in every sense of the word a slow, agonizing death sentence.[13]

In a testament to Victor's will, he and Dimitri survived the crossing's initial rigors and, subsequently, traveled several days in an uncovered truck with one hundred other prisoners, finally landing at a camp known for producing coal. They were both assigned to work the mines. Every day, Dimitri and

---

12   Goners.

13   Today, the Mask of Sorrow monument in Magadan commemorates all those who died in Kolyma's forced-labor camps.

his debilitated father were roused at four o'clock and, along with fifty other prisoners, marched through the snow to the mine accompanied by armed guards. Working the mines was a 24-hour, seven-day-a-week job, and Dimitri and Victor were assigned to the day shift. Dimitri was young, strong, and agile. He was given the job of emptying slag cars.

Slag, the unusable bedrock, had to be removed from the mines before the veins of coal could be harvested. He was responsible for emptying the railcars of slag and then sending the cars back to the mine. Dimitri became known around camp for the good work he did and held some favor with the camp's commander.

His father, however, was sent into the mine to harvest the precious coal. Wet with condensation from the natural water that ran through the mines, the possibility of a cave-in always loomed in the darkness. Prisoners became good at reading the mines and the sounds that could be a harbinger of collapse. Despite supports that were placed in the mine walls, cave-ins were a regular occurrence. The miners knew that stripping the bedrock out quicker than the supports could be placed was a recipe for disaster, but there were quotas to meet and severe penalties for failure. The only good thing about working inside the mine was that the men inside were given a larger bread ration than those on the outside. Dimitri always refused his father's offer to share his extra ration—he knew if his father was to survive, he would need to eat as much as possible. All the men received cabbage soup or kasha (buckwheat porridge), but both were mostly liquid broth with very little substance.

It was the same every day. Up at four in the morning, eat a piece of bread, and then march two miles to the mines. Work fourteen hours of hard labor, march back to camp, eat another piece of bread, and then lights out. It was easy to lose track of time in the camp. But, Mother Nature was not so easily distracted, and Dimitri could feel winter approaching. He knew his father would not survive the winter. Looking like death already, with sunken eyes, hollowed-out cheeks, and nothing but skin and bones, Victor was becoming a *dokhodyagi. His eyes give it away*, Dimitri thought. *They have lost their life.* Dimitri's greatest sorrow was that he could do nothing to help his father. Reciting the same prayer he said every night, Dimitri pleaded, "Dear God, if you are really out there, please take my father so that he can be with his beloved wife, my mother. He is of no further service to you here. Do not make him suffer. I pray you will hear me." He was not sure he believed in a God who allowed such misery to occur, but he also knew men sometimes found their God in the most miserable conditions.

As they neared the end of their first summer in Kolyma, Victor started coughing. At first, it was just a slight clearing of the throat, but a week later he was coughing up blood. The coal dust Victor had inhaled over the last three months was finally taking its toll. His weakened state left him with no reserves to fight off the pneumonitis that infected his lungs. The following week, he was gone. The night he died, Dimitri held his father in his arms and wept tears of grief, guilt, and relief. Holding his father, Dimitri quietly repeated the poem his mother had taught him,

> *The bosom of mother Russia*
> *Remains firm for all her children*
> *Do not cry for her, ye men of little faith.*
> *She will always be there, for you.*
> *Eat her berries and drink her water*
> *She provides these for your life.*
> *Walk her mountains, warm yourself in her sun.*
> *And when the stars come out*
> *Lay down your sleepy heads.*
> *And she will cradle you into the morn.*

In the morning, Dimitri spoke to the camp commander and requested permission to dig a grave for his father. Otherwise, he knew his father would be taken to the woods and left there for scavengers to desecrate. Fortunately, he had obtained some black market cigarettes, and for five cigarettes he was allowed to have a shift off to bury his father. It took him all day to dig a grave deep enough, but he was determined to place his father to rest with dignity.

Evening came, and, because he had not gone to work, he did not receive his bread ration for that day. For the first time in a long while, Dimitri allowed himself to think about his former life at home with his parents. After sobbing himself to sleep, his dreams were filled with darkness. In the morning, he awoke with a new resolve to honor his father's instructions. When he was done with his sentence, Dimitri swore he would return to Russia and expose these horrors. In the meantime, his only job was to survive. *I love you, Papa,* he thought as he readied himself for another excruciating day in the mines.

—

Dimitri spent three years working the mines until a local camp commander found out that he was literate. Once his secret was known, Dimitri was transferred to the commander's camp, where he was assigned to teach the commander's children how to read and write. The environment was less harsh, and the commander fed and clothed him so that he was presentable to the children. He stayed there until his ten-year sentence was completed, and he was released. On the day that he left Kolyma, Dimitri noted with irony that it was the very same train that had brought him to such misery that would now deliver him back to

Moscow to start a new life. It was the end of 1953, and he was twenty-four years old.

CHAPTER VIII

There is no greater agony than bearing
an untold story inside of you.

—MAYA ANGELOU

WASHINGTON, DC
2011-EARLY 2012

Elena walked into the studio through the back door, quickly glancing in an entryway mirror as she pulled the loose ends of her long auburn hair behind her ears and noted that she looked tired. Entering through the back meant she was less likely to disturb ongoing classes, and she really didn't want to answer the inevitable questions about whether they had found her father. Everyone in the studio knew and loved Dimitri. He was like a great-grandfather to all of her students and their parents. Parents loved listening to his stories of Russia and his life there. It was almost as if they thought he was a secret agent or some such nonsense. Elena did not understand their fascination with him, but she was grateful for their diverted attention whenever he was in the studio.

"Miss Elena, Miss Elena," she heard a child call. "Watch me. I can do a pirouette just like you."

Smiling, Elena went into the studio area to watch the little girl perform one perfect pirouette. "Very good, Jennifer. Excellent! Next week, we will look for two pirouettes, *da*?"

The little girl smiled at her teacher's approval and continued practicing. Jennifer's mother approached Elena.

"Is your father all right, Elena?" she asked in a whisper of concern.

"Oh yes, they found him, and he is back to his usual cranky self." Elena smiled reassuringly. "Not sure what I am going to do with him."

"Well, if you ever want to give him away, we would be happy to take him. Jennifer just loves him, and so does my husband," she said. Elena knew she was only half joking.

"Oh Krista, you are too kind. Be careful what you wish for though. I might take you up on it." Elena smiled and walked over to answer the ringing phone.

The truth was Elena adored the studio parents and students as much as they loved her. She took great pleasure in making the studio comfortable for her students and their families. Her attention to detail endeared her to many. She made sure that each student received her attention whenever they came in, even if they had a lesson with another teacher. Her goal was to bring the beauty of dance to life for each student. Adult students who took lessons learned from her and Andrei. They envied the beautiful lines and moves the two of them were able to create together. Students worked hard to emulate their grace. People often stayed long after their lessons just to spend time with Elena and the others in the studio. It had taken several years of hard work, but it was now a place of community for many people.

Deciding to stay in the Washington, D.C. area after graduating from college, Elena jumped at the opportunity to buy the studio with Andrei as her business partner. The people in D.C. appreciated the fine arts, and the pair was often sought out to perform at conventions, private parties, and theater events. These were not her favorite venues, but it helped pay the bills. She and Andrei captivated audiences with their romantic waltzes and steamy boleros, and, for a few minutes of performance time, they walked away with a hefty check.

In fact, she met her husband, Jack, during one such performance. She and Andrei did a show for the USO, and he was the officer in charge that day. It was a chance meeting, and their first encounter had been a bit rough. But, the chemistry between them had been instant, and they became inseparable.

Jack was stateside at the time and spent as much time with her as he could. Elena loved that he could make her laugh and found the stories of his adventures in the military exciting and arousing. They had a whirlwind romance of theater dates, military balls, and Elena's favorite ballet performances. She thought he was the bravest man she had ever met and took great comfort in his authoritative personality. It was nice to have someone else make decisions for her, and she trusted him. After six months, they decided to elope. Dimitri was livid with Elena at the time. "Lena, he is not right for you," was all he would say.

But she was sure she had found her soulmate, and she was head over heels in love. However, not long after the wedding, Jack's personality began to change. His mood became increasingly dark, and he was restless and easily irritated. Elena attributed it to stress in his medical career and did her best to accommodate his mood swings. Six months after the wedding, she became pregnant. Thrilled with the news, she was sure this would bring Jack out of his doldrums and reinvigorate their relationship. Unfortunately, it did not, and Jack announced he was returning to Afghanistan for a yearlong deployment almost immediately after. It was hard to hide her disappointment, but she made the best of it by writing to him almost daily. She received very few letters in return.

The pregnancy was difficult. Carrying twins is never an easy endeavor, and for the last five months of her pregnancy, she was forbidden to dance. This prohibition only added to her poor mood and depression. Andrei did what he could to cheer her up. Consulting with his students, at his invitation, lifted her spirits briefly. He would often place a fresh bouquet, from the flower shop around the corner, on her credenza. It was Andrei who went to Lamaze classes with her and Andrei who was there with her for the birth of her twins when they arrived four weeks early.

Finally, she reached Jack via Skype two weeks after the births.

"Two! Elena, you didn't tell me you were having twins!"

"Jack, don't be silly, of course I told you. Did you not read any of my letters? I've filled those letters with news about the babies for the last nine months."

Elena saw the black anger rise in his face. "Elena, I'm in a fucking war zone over here. Do you really think I have time to read the pages and pages of letters that you send me? I'm over here trying to stay alive. I have more important things on my mind than your pregnancy," Jack said, looking at the screen angrily, his voice full of derision. "You need to stop sending me all this shit! The guys here keep asking me what is wrong with you. You know what, Elena? I don't have any idea what's wrong with you except that you are a pain in my ass. That's what's wrong with you."

"Jack . . . please don't . . . " she said, unable to hold back the tears. She didn't understand his irritation and anger.

"Get over it, Elena. How do you think the twins are going to feel when their father doesn't come home? What are you going to tell them then? That you purposely tried to keep me from leaving by getting pregnant? And now you have two kids to manage and no husband?"

"Jack, why are you saying these things? Of course you are coming home! We love you . . . "

"Elena, you need to leave me alone. This conversation is over." The screen went blank.

Sobbing uncontrollably and stunned by his complete disregard for their babies, she thought, *He didn't even ask what their names were.* Her new reality was a cruel, unexpected one.

After her conversation with Jack, Elena fell victim to postpartum depression, and her nights became sleepless. She became thin and withdrawn. Andrei and Dimitri worried about her and kept a close eye on her. Fortunately, Dimitri, Andrei, and the rest of the studio staff fell in love with her twins, and there was no lack of attention or help. Everyone took turns changing diapers and feeding and playing with the kids. Dimitri hovered over them, a doting grandfather. Andrei built them a beautiful mobile with pictures of Elena, Dimitri, and Jack twirling to Brahms's lullaby. Their first year growing up in the studio was filled with love and adoration. With Dimitri and Andrei keeping close tabs on her, Elena slowly came out of her depression. By the time of their first birthday, the twins and their mother were thriving. *I wish your father could see how much you guys have grown*, she thought at their birthday gathering.

Elena continued to send Jack letters with pictures of the twins and news of their accomplishments, but since the disastrous Skype call there had been no response. But, the twins brought a new joy and focus to her life, and, for that, she was grateful. However, the truth of her failing marriage weighed heavily on her.

As the twins turned fourteen months old, Jack returned from Afghanistan physically unscathed but emotionally unavailable and dark. Distant, restless, and moody, he was volatile and unpredictable. Lena tried talking to him, but he usually just cut her off with a harsh comment. Leaving the house for hours on end was his way of escaping the need for conversation. He often came home late at night very drunk. Worse, yet, were his uncontrollable rages. Lena was beginning to fear Jack's erratic behavior.

One afternoon she was getting the children ready to go to the park and asked Jack to come with them.

"Jack, do you want to go to the park with us? It's a gorgeous day, we could take a picnic if you want," she asked from the kitchen, being very careful to keep her tone sweet. She was learning to identify which tones or pitches in her voice set him off.

Jack came into the kitchen from the living room. He looked terrible—red eyes, sunken cheeks, unshaven, wearing only a T-shirt and jeans. He smelled terrible.

"Oh honey, I'm sorry, I didn't realize you were sleeping. Do you want us to wait while you get cleaned up, or should we go without you?" Elena asked, her gut knotted up in a tight ball, shoulders tense, waiting for his reaction.

"Who the hell do you think you are? I'm in there trying to sleep, and all I can hear is you banging around this kitchen, singing and laughing. What the hell is so funny, Elena? You got someone out here that's making you laugh? Don't you think I know what's going on? You're going to meet your lover, aren't you?" Jack said as he slammed his fist onto the counter. Picking up a glass, he threw it to the floor and walked over to Elena, grabbing her jacket and lifting her off the floor. "Don't think I won't kill you both." He let go of her and returned to the living room.

Elena shook so badly she could barely stand, and the twins shrieked with fear. She knew she had to get out of there with the children. She grabbed her purse and left. Instead of going to the park, she called a taxi from her cell phone and arranged to stay in a hotel. Terrified and almost frozen in fear of her husband, she did not know what to do. When she did return home the next day, Jack acted as if nothing had happened. From then on, Lena left him to do his own thing as much as possible.

Just before the twins turned two, Jack informed Elena that he was returning to Afghanistan. Protesting, Elena replied, "But Jack, you've only been home for a few months, and you've barely spent any time with the children. Do you really have to go so soon?"

"Elena, I can't take you anymore. You're constantly nagging me, and I'm sick of you trying to control me. I didn't ask for these kids. They're your problem, not mine. I'm going back home—I mean I'm going back to Afghanistan. At least there I know what I'm getting, and it won't be a controlling bitch with two kids!" Though she'd adjusted to his behavior over the last several months, he was still able to cut her to the quick with his rage.

Later the same day, Dimitri came to the studio to see the twins. He could see Lena had been crying and inquired as to why. Lena confided in him, "Papa, I am ashamed to say this, but I think you might have been right about my marriage."

"*Pochemu*, Lena?"[14] he asked as he put his arm around her shoulders.

---

14 "Why, Lena?"

"Papa, Jack is leaving. He's going back to Afghanistan, again. I asked why he would go so soon, and he told me I was too controlling and miserable to live with. Papa, he has barely looked at his children, and, when he is home, he spends all his time on the computer. He won't eat with us, and, Papa, he does not come to bed with me. I find him on the couch in the morning. He has been so angry, Papa . . . I am afraid of him," Lena confessed with tears streaming down her face. "The worst part is—I know he volunteered to go back. Papa, do you think there is someone else?" she sobbed.

"*Moy ziechick*, I am so sorry to see how sad you are," Dimitri said as he wrapped his arms around his daughter. "Why haven't you come to me and told me about this?"

"I know, Papa, I should have, but . . . I kept thinking as time went on he would come back to us. He would be the man I fell in love with."

"Elena, perhaps this is an effect of his war experience. My father once told me that war sometimes robs men of their dignity and their minds. Maybe Jack has . . . what do they call it . . . PTSD?"

Considering the possibility, Elena said, "Papa, I never thought that he might be hurting inside. He has always been so strong. But, maybe you're right. Maybe he just needs some time. But, why go back to the place that is hurting you? Why wouldn't you stay with your wife and children who love you and try to heal from the pain?"

"Elena, maybe it is the only thing he knows. Maybe war is his comfort zone, his home, just like the studio is your home."

"Papa, I hope you are wrong because eventually this war is going to end. Then what?"

"I don't know, Lena. I don't know."

Elena took some comfort in her father's insight and tried to suppress her fears. Perhaps the physical chemistry between her and Jack had overwhelmed both of them and their good sense. Maybe their marriage had been too impulsive. *Tying Jack down was like trying to capture the wind*, Elena thought. Secretly, in the back of her mind, she was a little relieved he was leaving. His volatility was escalating, and she feared for herself and the twins.

Three weeks later, Jack was back in Afghanistan.

CHAPTER IX

Only the dead have seen the end of war.

—PLATO

WASHINGTON, DC
JANUARY 2, 2013

It was ten months to the day since Jack had left. The morning had started like any other for Elena. The kids were ready for the day. Everyone was fed and dressed. Elena sighed and thought to herself, *When Jack gets back, this will be easier . . . I hope.* Reviewing her plans for the day, which included multiple lessons at the studio and practice with Andrei later, lifted her spirits. Smiling, she thought, *Andrei is going to kill me, but I'm going to have to get the kids first, before practice.* She collected the twins and put them in their car seats.

Dropping the twins off at daycare was pretty simple. The facility was located just a block from the studio, which was a huge convenience. Elena could run over to check on them during her breaks. The owner was a young woman with a degree in childhood education. Like Elena, she had decided to create a business for herself instead of working for someone else. Elena admired Miss Laura and liked her staff. It was the perfect arrangement.

After dropping the twins off, Elena made a quick stop at Costco to pick up supplies for the studio. Usually she ordered online, but they had just run out of a few things. *Let's see . . . toilet paper, staples, paper clips, cleaning supplies, and what else?* There was one more thing she needed, but she couldn't remember. So, she checked out and left for the studio.

As was her usual habit, she went in through the back door. After brewing a cup of coffee, she flopped into her desk chair and grabbed her organizer to go over her schedule for the day while she drank her coffee. She liked a latte in the morning and had been so pleased when Andrei brought a special coffee maker into the studio. Since then it was her daily routine to have a latte, organize her lessons, and enjoy five minutes of peace before the day truly started. Luck was with her that day, as she was able to slip into the office without anyone noticing her. It was quiet, anyway, as the new year holidays were just ending, and people were still away or had family in town.

Elena heard the front door open. The bell she had hung on the door always announced an arrival. She knew whoever was out front would handle the preliminaries and ask her student to get warmed up. As she stood up, Andrei appeared in the doorway.

"Elena, I have two gentlemen here that need to speak to you."

Elena barely registered the strange look on his face. "Andrei, I can't. I have a lesson that's just about to start."

"No, Lena, not right now you don't." He stepped aside, and two very official-looking Army officers entered the doorway.

"Mrs. Foster? Would you please have a seat?" the taller officer asked.

Elena felt her stomach tighten and a chill ran through her, which she tried to ignore. "OK guys, I have already donated money and time to the USO this year."

"No ma'am, that's not why we are here. Please . . . if you would, sit down," the officer repeated.

Elena complied, and he continued.

"Mrs. Foster, I have been asked to inform you that your husband, Lieutenant Commander Jack Foster, was reported dead in Kandahar, Afghanistan, at 0100 on January 1, 2013. He was killed by an IED while on a mission. On behalf of the Secretary of Defense, I extend to you and your family my deepest sympathy for your great loss."

Elena tried to tell herself it must be a mistake. *I just talked to him at Christmas*, she thought. It had not been a pleasant conversation, but at least he had called and spoken to the twins. She said it out loud. "But I just spoke to my husband on Christmas." She could feel all her strength leave her body.

"Yes ma'am, I understand," the officer replied as gently as possible. "I am so sorry to have to deliver this news to you. Is there someone you would like us to call? Is there someone who should be here with you?"

Elena saw Andrei standing to the side, quietly watching and listening. "No, officer, I'll take care of her," he said as Elena looked over at him. He moved behind her chair and put his hand on her shoulder. The officers asked her if she had any other questions.

Elena was speechless, but Andrei asked, "What about his remains? What happens next?"

The officer explained that Jack's remains would be shipped home and that he could be buried in Arlington Cemetery, if Elena so desired. His remains were due to arrive within the next week. There would be official documentation to file, but he would be afforded an official military burial.

"Your husband died a hero, ma'am. He died trying to save another soldier. Please know that we will be available to help you through this process. There will be someone contacting you with information regarding when his remains will be returned, and we will pick you up and take you to the airport when they arrive. We are here to serve you in your time of need. Please feel free to call me at any time." He put several of his cards on the desk.

"Is there anything we can do for you right now, ma'am?" the other officer asked.

Elena just shook her head.

"May God bless you, ma'am, and again, please accept our condolences." With that they turned and left.

Elena looked at Andrei, an expression of disbelief still on her face. Andrei walked out of the office for a brief moment and returned as she remained staring into space.

"Elena, I asked Jackie to cancel lessons for today and tomorrow. Let's go get the kids and get you home."

As she stood up, she said, "Andrei, before we get the kids, I have to tell Papa. He would want to know."

"OK then," he said with a sigh. "Let's go tell Dema, and, then, we'll get the kids."

When he heard the news, all Dimitri could say was, "I'm so sorry, Lena." He took her in his arms and held her as she cried. The staff at Harbor Place later reported that Dimitri was visibly disturbed after she left and that he became disruptive and confused.

Over the next two weeks, Elena was swamped with military paperwork. She must have filled out twenty forms, dug deep into her files to find the proper documentation requested, and was instructed in military protocol concerning the military funeral she had requested for Jack. As promised, the military picked Elena up in an official vehicle and took her to the tarmac so that she could be there when the casket was unloaded and placed in the hearse. It was a frigid day, and there was slush and ice everywhere. The plane had arrived late due to weather. As the casket was unloaded, Elena shivered in the cold. The reality of Jack's death set in as the bearers unloaded the coffin. Once the casket was safely placed in the hearse, it was taken to a military holding area until funeral arrangements were completed.

At the end of a very long two weeks, it was finally time for the funeral. She had chosen Arlington Cemetery. She felt Jack deserved that. Upon arrival, she, Andrei, Dimitri, and the twins were escorted to a set of folding chairs set up in front of the gravesite. Elena had been somewhat reluctant to bring Dimitri, but he had asked about the service and wanted to be there with her.

The weather had improved slightly, and the sun was out. But, the air was still frosty, and the twins cuddled up to Dimitri for warmth. As the service began, six men in dress uniform carried the casket, draped with the American flag, to the gravesite. They reverently placed their fallen comrade's casket on the support in front of the grave. Once relieved of their precious cargo, they stepped aside. Since Jack was Catholic, a priest read the funeral rites. After the priest concluded his reading, three riflemen with M16s fired a three-volley salute. When done, they presented arms in honor of Jack.

Elena maintained her composure until "Taps" was sounded. The haunting sound of that simple melody found its way into the hole in her heart, and the tears spilled. Trembling, she watched as the honor guard collected the flag and began to fold it. The officer who had been assisting her told her the flag would be folded thirteen times, representing the original thirteen colonies. At the very end, the flag would be folded to resemble the tri-cornered hat the colonial military had worn back in the Revolution.

Elena fought to regain her composure before the officer presented her with the flag. She saw the flag handed off to the senior officer in the honor guard. He walked over to Elena, bent down on one knee, and said, "On behalf of the President of the United States . . . and a grateful nation, please accept this flag as a symbol of our appreciation for your husband's honorable and faithful service."

"Thank you," Elena said as she accepted the flag from him with tears rolling down her cheeks. He stood and led the rest of the honor guard off the field. And, with that, it was done. She was a forty-five-year-old widow with twins and a father with progressively worsening dementia. All she could see at that moment was darkness.

Andrei drove them back to Elena's house, where she received many people throughout the rest of the day offering their condolences—people from the studio, Jack's stateside military friends, hospital personnel who had worked with Jack the physician, and some people she didn't know. Dimitri talked with many of the guests, freeing Elena to stand in a receiving line. It was very late in the day when the final guest left. Collapsing on the couch, she looked up at Andrei and let out a huge sigh.

"Lena." Andrei sat down beside her on the couch and put his arm around her. "Do you want me to take Dema back?"

"Oh, I don't know, Andrei. He's been so good to have here today. The twins have loved having him, and he did a really great job of talking with people. This is the wonderful side of him. Why can't it always be like this?" she asked as she buried herself into the comfort of his arm. "Papa," she called out. "What do you want to do tonight? Do you want to stay with me or go back to Harbor Place?"

Dimitri emerged from the other room, where he had been watching cartoons with the twins. "*Moy ziechick*, I will stay with you as long as you want." The twins came clamoring in after him.

"Stay here, stay here," they shouted as they tugged on his hands.

Laughing, Andrei said, "OK, I guess that's your answer. Why not? The kids are having a great time with him. I will feel better if you have someone here with you tonight, anyway. Let me help you clean up a little, and then I'll leave."

Elena looked up at him and felt a huge wave of gratitude. It seemed like he was always there when she needed him. Always.

"*Spaciba*, Andrei, but you must be exhausted. Go home. I can clean up. It will help to keep my mind distracted."

"I'll stay until you get the kids to bed. Besides, let's make sure Dema is going to be OK."

"OK, deal," Elena said weakly.

Over the next couple of hours, she and Andrei got the place picked up, gave the twins a bath, and got them to bed. Dimitri fell asleep in the other room watching TV. Sitting on the couch for a breather, Elena started to reminisce.

"Andrei, do you remember the day we met Jack?" she asked softly.

Sitting down next to her, Andrei said, "Of course I do. It was after a Christmas Eve show, wasn't it, at the USO?"

"*Da*, we were looking for the officer in charge to pick up our check for the performance that night. Remember one of the soldiers sent us down some long hallway to his office?"

"Yes, and when we knocked, he barked out 'ENTER' like some mad dog," Andrei replied.

"When we walked in, there was Jack leaning back in his chair with his long legs up on the desk, smoking a cigar. I immediately noticed his eyes . . . they were so blue. And, then, when he saw us, he practically jumped out of his chair in an attempt to look dignified."

"'Good evening, ma'am, what can I do for you?' was all he could muster," Andrei said, smiling at the memory. "And then you said . . . "

"'Are you the officer in charge?'" Elena said.

"Then we said we were told to see him about the check for the performance."

"'Oh! You guys were the entertainment for tonight's show. Sorry, my mind was on something else,'" Elena said, trying to imitate Jack's voice.

"The next thing you know, he's giving us some BS about ACCTCOM not bringing the checks over. We were so disappointed. I think we both had that money earmarked for Christmas shopping the next day," Andrei said.

"He did supposedly try to find us before the show and tell us. Remember we arrived just in time for the show because of that huge traffic jam? I decided to cut him some slack." Elena laughed.

"Slack?" Andrei questioned and looked at Elena with a puzzled face. "Lena, I thought you were going to reach across his desk and choke him."

"Oh, well, then he said, 'Ma'am, I promise you I will deliver it myself tomorrow. Where and when should I bring it to you?'" Lena said trying again to imitate Jack's deep voice.

Andrei and Lena both laughed.

"Then you warned him not to be late," Andrei said. "'Yes ma'am, no ma'am, I won't be late, I will see you tomorrow at 1300 hours . . . That's one o'clock your time, ma'am,'" Andrei continued in his best imitation of Jack's voice. "Then you almost jumped down his throat. 'Soldier, I am well aware of what 1300 hours means!'"

"And then before we left, I asked him his name," Elena said.

"'Oh, sorry ma'am, yes ma'am, Lieutenant Commander Jack Foster at your service, ma'am,'" Andrei responded.

"And once we got into the car, we laughed so hard about what an arrogant jerk he was. Then, you told me that you noticed he couldn't take his eyes off me." Elena smiled.

"Yes, Elena, I remember. It's a good memory. Hold on to it. Your children will want to hear it someday."

"Yes." She smiled weakly. "I agree. But, you know, Andrei, lately I've been thinking that our marriage wasn't going to make it. The last time he was home, it was awful. He felt like a complete stranger. He barely looked at the twins. It broke my heart to watch them climb all over him and know that he couldn't care less. I told Papa about it. He thought maybe Jack was suffering from PTSD. But, really I think he just didn't want to be tied down."

"I knew something was wrong. I could see it in your eyes, and hear it in your voice, Elena. I'm sorry. It must have been very hard to have him here and not be able to take comfort in each other."

"I will never forget how coldly he looked at me whenever I tried to talk to him. It was as if he didn't even know me, like I was an intruder! But, Andrei, I had just had his children, shouldn't that have meant something?" Elena's voice jumped in pitch.

"Shh, shh, Lena," he said as he stroked the hair off of her forehead. "You will never know what was going on in his head."

Letters of Forgiveness

She looked up at Andrei and suddenly felt her exhaustion from the day. "Andrei, I don't know how to thank you for all you have done . . . I can't imagine how I would have done this without you." They stood up together to walk to the door.

At the door, Andrei wrapped his arms around her and pulled her tightly to him. "You will never be alone, Lena. I am always here for you." He kissed her cheek and said goodbye.

Elena shook her head as he walked down the sidewalk. *Thank God for that man*, she thought and closed the door. Too tired to find her way upstairs to the bedroom, she slept on the couch that night.

Katy, Dimitri, & Elena

CHAPTER X

____

When the student is ready, the teacher will appear.

—BUDDHA

Twelve hours after the disastrous mission, Katy was in an ICU bed at Bagram Airfield Hospital. Bagram had been built by the Russians in 1980, but after their retreat from Afghanistan it had fallen into shambles. After 9/11, American forces rebuilt the facility. Now, Bagram was a bustling city spanning six thousand acres with all the westernized hallmarks of home. Large airfields dominated the landscape, with huts, tents, and formal dormitories lining the periphery. Gyms, Pizza Huts, Subways, and even a Popeyes made Bagram feel very much like home.

Bagram was also home to a detention facility where suspected Taliban and al-Qaeda fighters were detained. But, more importantly, Bagram was a Level I trauma center for treating severely injured troops.

Katy awoke to multiple IV lines in her arms and drains coming from her left leg. She was being transfused. *I must have lost blood*, she thought, *but why*? As her eyes adjusted to her new surroundings, memories of the night before flared like small exploding grenades. She thought her heart was going to jump out of her chest, it was pounding so hard. And, she could hear herself breathing rapidly. *Was it real? Did Jack die out there in my arms? Is Shveta really gone?* It was too horrific to believe. *Maybe it's just a terrible nightmare*, she thought. *When I wake up, they both will be sitting right next to me.* Trying to decipher what was real and what was drug-induced was difficult. Her eyes were heavy, and she allowed herself a moment to close them. That moment turned into another twelve hours.

—

It was the searing pain in her leg that finally forced her awake. She screamed as the pain connected with her awakening brain. Immediately, she was given more morphine by a nurse. *Oh, Jack, Shveta. I'm so sorry. I should have saved you both*, she thought as her nightmare registered as reality. Quickly, the morphine took her to a place where nightmares couldn't follow.

Letters of Forgiveness

When she finally came to, she was being loaded onto a C-17 carrier headed for Landstuhl Regional Medical Center. She and twelve others were being flown back to the US military base in Germany for further intensive medical treatment. There would be no opportunity to say goodbye to her colleagues back in Kandahar. No shared grieving with her friends over those lost that night. No time for memorials and, worse, no opportunity to say goodbye to Jack. She wanted to touch his desk one more time, sit in the chair he sat in, smell his uniform jacket, collect a piece of memorabilia from their affair. The journal and pen she had picked out for him on R&R, the book on his shelf that he had promised her when he was done, or even the little toy sailboat they had built together out of popsicle sticks. They had planned to rent a sailboat and sail the East Coast on the Intercoastal Waterway when they returned stateside. The silent tears running down her face betrayed her broken heart and grief.

The ride to Landstuhl was bumpy and long, but liberal use of pain medication kept her constantly drifting in and out during the long ride. The next several weeks followed a similar pattern, waking up in pain, receiving more drugs, and then sleeping in a morphine-induced euphoria. When Katy was wounded, she lost a lot of blood, and ground-in dirt and shrapnel had caused a serious infection in her leg. She underwent multiple surgeries to clear out the infection as well as several rounds of antibiotics.

But after multiple attempts at trying to clear her system of infection, it was clear that she was going to need an amputation above the knee to keep it from spreading and killing her. After the amputation at Landstuhl, she was transferred back to the states and sent to Walter Reed Hospital in Washington, D.C.

—

At Walter Reed, Katy sank into a web of darkness and despair. Her bubbly, can-do personality changed after Kandahar. She was more of a raging bull now. Her mood was foul, and it took very little to set her off. She screamed at the nurses and aides, who tried to help her, for no apparent reason. She was cruelest to the hydrotherapy staff, accusing them of trying to kill her whenever they brought her in for her treatments. She was inconsolable. The pain in her leg was relentless, but the time had come to cut back on the morphine she was using. The staff at Walter Reed recognized PTSD when they saw it, and they referred Katy to an in-house psychiatrist who wanted her to come to group three times a week.

"That's not going to happen, Doc," she said.

"Why not, Katy? What are you afraid will happen?" he asked.

"I'm not fucking afraid of anything, but I'm not going to sit around and whine and cry while you expose the demons in my head to everyone. I can figure this out on my own!" She turned around and wheeled herself out of the psychiatrist's office. She was, however, still required to attend group sessions, where she sat for forty-five minutes, three times a week, in insolent silence.

Meanwhile, she continued to wake screaming from dreams filled with blood and death. The slightest unexpected noise sent her into a state of hypervigilance, and her skin crawled with what felt like thousands of tiny ants. Frightened by her lack of control, Katy eyed everything and everyone with deep suspicion. She couldn't understand why she wasn't allowed a weapon at her bedside. "How the fuck do you expect me to protect myself?" she screamed at a nurse who confiscated a knife she had hidden away.

The psychiatrist asked over and over again, "Second Lieutenant, exactly what are you afraid is going to happen to you here?"

"Nothing," came her insolent response.

"You know you are safe, right? You have left the war far behind. You have nothing left to fear here."

"Says who?" Katy asked.

She was on multiple antidepressants, but all they did was make her sleep or, worse yet, feel numb. "I would rather be dead than be this numb," Katy told another patient, and a nurse who overheard her reported the comment. They placed her on suicide watch, which meant she could only use plastic utensils for meals and had someone with her at all times, even at night, which only contributed to her insomnia. Katy decided she would take her Prozac and Abilify. This seemed to appease the staff, and she came off suicide watch.

—

It was Katy's sixth week in Walter Reed Hospital.

"Ma'am, it's time for your hydrotherapy," the aid entering the day room said with a smile.

Katy hated him for that smile. She hated the nurses and her doctors. She hated the Army for sending her there. Most of all she hated herself.

"I don't feel like going. I'm really not up for it today," she said meekly, thinking this might put him off.

"Sorry, ma'am, doctor's orders."

"Screw the goddamn doctors. I don't care, I'm not going!" she screamed at him.

Just as she said this, the nurse came in with morphine to medicate her while she was in the baths. She pushed the medication through the IV, and, despite Katy's attempt to resist the effect, she instantly fell prey to the rapture of the drug. Her eyes glazed over, her breathing slowed, and a hazy fog clouded her brain. Her last coherent thought was about escaping Walter Reed.

The orderly gently lifted her onto the stretcher, and she was wheeled into the hydrotherapy bath. Hydrotherapy, a form of wound debridement, removes dead tissue to make room for new growth. To Katy, it was torture. Every other day, some massive hulk of an aide would pick up her tiny body, place her in a whirlpool of circulating water, and apply various topical medications. It hurt like hell as the necrotic skin over the wound infection was blasted off by the water. Katy knew hydrotherapy was helping her leg, but her pain during the baths was unbearable even with painkillers. However, everyone except Katy knew her pain went much deeper than the skin on her leg.

Returning to her room, and still feeling the effects of the morphine and warm bath, she slept the rest of the afternoon. The next few days were filled with painful attempts at fittings for a prosthesis. She couldn't tolerate the prosthesis for more than a few moments and was completely unable to bear weight on it. Part of it was the pain, but part of it was her insolent, unforgiving attitude. That "go-get 'em, I can do anything" personality had been lost in the desert of Kandahar, and it didn't look like it was coming back anytime soon.

—

After eight weeks at Walter Reed, Katy's doctors and physical therapist decided that Katy needed long-term rehab despite her protests.

"Katy," Dr. White said, "After a lot of discussion, we feel it's in your best interest to be discharged to continue your rehab in a skilled facility. You no longer need constant nursing care. In fact, you need intense physical therapy, and we can't offer that here."

"What?" Katy shot back. "Why? Why do you think I will do any better there than in this hellhole? I don't want to go to rehab, and I won't. Listen, I gave up my leg for you people. The least you can do is take care of me," she screamed.

"Katy," he replied with a sigh, "that is exactly what we are trying to do. The decision is made. Do you have any further questions?"

"No, I'm not going! Get the fuck out of my room, you worthless bastard."

While she hated Walter Reed, she also did not want to leave its familiarity and felt that her discharge to another facility was a betrayal. Although she could not see it, with her sleep haunted by nightmares and her days a slugfest, trying desperately to avoid the abyss of deep depression, she needed someplace to provide her with long-term care.

CHAPTER XI

There are always flowers for those who want to see them.
—HENRI MATISSE

HARBOR PLACE
WASHINGTON, D.C.
MARCH 2013

It was mid-March when she arrived at Harbor Place in the Village. Harbor Place was a unique facility. It housed both a nursing home with a dementia unit and a rehab facility. They had a longstanding contract with Veterans Affairs to provide acute rehabilitation services. The facility had a good reputation, and its beds stayed filled. Getting into Harbor Place was a stroke of luck for Katy, although she didn't think so at the time.

During the admission process, an elderly gentleman from the memory unit wandered into the administrative offices and started talking to Katy as she waited to be processed. At first, she didn't realize that he wasn't making any sense. She thought she had heard him wrong.

"I'm sorry, sir, are you talking to me?" she asked, feeling edgy as the stranger came closer. She looked to see if there was anyone else around.

"Pretty lady, butterflies fly, butterflies fly," was all that she could make out of the stream of gibberish.

"Sir, I'm sorry, I can't help you," she said, increasing her personal space by backing the wheelchair up against the wall. Again, she looked around to see if she could determine where he had come from and who should be watching out for this guy.

"Oh, Henry, there you are!" screeched a very heavyset African American woman dressed in street clothes. She had a set of keys around her neck and a badge that said, "Nancy, RN, Memory Unit." "They don't usually get off the floor, but this one is a sly dog," she said, smiling. She took Henry's hand gently and coaxed him to go with her. As they left the room, Henry turned and looked at Katy.

"Butterflies fly," he said again.

Katy just shook her head. "Good Lord, what kind of looney bin did they send me to?" she said under her breath.

"Sometimes, it can be a real looney bin, I'm afraid, but don't worry. The part of the facility you are going to be in is nowhere near our memory unit," said the registrar, who appeared out of nowhere. Katy was embarrassed that she had been overheard.

The registrar held a clipboard with a very official Harbor Place decal on the back. She looked about six feet tall from where Katy sat, but everyone looked tall when you were in a wheelchair. She was blond with a beautiful smile that Katy thought was phony. *Don't waste that cheerful bullshit on me. I know what this place is,* she thought.

"So, Ms. Glass, I have several papers you need to sign, financial and payment agreements, privacy policy, and an acknowledgement of our rules and regulation pamphlet that I will be giving you," the lady said cheerfully.

"Cut the crap, this is all paperwork to make sure someone is responsible for the bill. Well, I can tell you, I am not paying for this place. I don't want to be here, and I'm not taking responsibility for it," Katy replied.

"Oh, Ms. Glass, I think you will really like it here—"

Katy cut her off before she could finish. "As I told my parents, I don't need this place, and I won't be participating in any therapy."

The blonde replied with a snip, "Apparently, they disagreed with you," and walked away with her clipboard.

As she walked away, Katy's parents, who had flown from California to help their daughter transition, came around the corner into the office.

"Mom, Dad, please don't make me do this. It's not going to help. I just need some time alone, at home."

But both her parents knew how troubled she was and refused to capitulate.

Seeing that she was fighting a losing battle, she agreed to stay if she could have a private room. "I'll be damned if I'm going to share this with anyone," she said to her parents, gesturing toward her missing leg. "I will go, but I need privacy. Promise me that and fine . . . I'll go," she said, negotiating her way with them. Her parents were all too happy to cover the cost of a private room if she would agree to stay.

Her room faced the inner courtyard atrium, and the aide who showed her to her room opened the curtains and very excitedly pointed out the garden view. "What you see here, ma'am, is just the beginning of the garden. Wait until the spring blooms come. You are going to be amazed."

Harbor Place was known for its courtyard gardens. Designed specifically to be wheelchair accessible, the glass atrium housed a number of different gardens. At the eastern end of the yard, closest to Katy's window, was the rose garden. Fragrant blooms of every conceivable color of garden rose hybrid teas, floribundas, grand floras, and more, were planted to the east. Irises, day lilies, English ivy, and other native plants provided a backdrop for the roses. A large cast of Michelangelo's David was flanked by enormous orange blossom bushes. In the middle of the rose garden, surrounded by climbing roses on a trellis, sat a concrete bench. Across the pathway, towards the north end of the atrium, was the Japanese serenity garden, complete with a meditative sand garden. Multiple Asian sculptures, planted discreetly within the greenery, lent an authentic flair to the space. At the very end of the walkway stood a mature cherry blossom tree. Underneath this tree was another relaxing place to sit. Leaving the meditation garden required crossing a Japanese bridge that traversed the man-made stream that ran through the entire atrium. Filled with smooth river rocks, the water looked like brilliant crystal running across them. The rush of the water over the rocks also created a sound like handbells. Wind chimes, glass ornaments, and air plants hung from trees on transparent wires, creating a look of whimsical fantasy. The garden's southwest end was filled with various walking paths that were covered by a large trellis that housed climbing vines of wisteria, bougainvillea, and hanging plants. Benches placed discreetly for quiet conversation or meditation were everywhere.

The stream completed its roundabout course in the middle of the atrium, ending in a beautiful waterfall. Built out of large brown slates placed on top of each other at various angles, the waterfall stood ten feet tall. The north end of the stream fed into the waterfall, and the water fell into a large pond filled with koi of various shapes and colors. After leaving the koi pond, the water fed the stream meandering south through the rest of the garden, ending in a reflection pool. The constant gurgling sound of falling water could be heard throughout the atrium. At night the waterfall lit up with colored lights. The rest of the garden also had small twinkling lights spread throughout the trees and foliage. It was a fanciful yet tranquil environment that Harbor Place had built for its residents, and the staff was very proud of their piece of paradise.

As the aide finished talking up the garden, Katy thought to herself, *Who the hell cares? I am not at all interested. Flowers are not going to make this any better.* "Thank you, I appreciate the information. Now, my parents are probably looking for me. Could you please go find them?" Katy said rudely, gesturing dismissively with her hand. As soon as the aide left the room, she closed the curtains.

"All I want is to be left alone!" she yelled at the closed door. Later that afternoon, she said goodbye to her parents and assured them she would give this her best effort. Once she saw them leave, she went back to her room, feeling very agitated. She remembered her time at Walter Reed and how much she had hated it there. *This place isn't going to be any friggin' different, is it?* she thought.

On her first night at Harbor Place, bombs, mortars, fire, and blood filled her dreams, and she woke shaking and sweating. Upon waking, she was immediately confused by her surroundings, but, then, she remembered. *Oh yeah . . . Harbor Place.* Sitting up on the bed and transferring to her wheelchair, she left her room. Wheeling out into the empty hall, she noticed there were no nurses patrolling the halls or aides to redirect her. She pushed herself a little farther and came upon the great room.

The great room was where meals were served and entertainment was provided. A large TV on the wall provided residents with a gathering point. Small tables with chairs and a few armchairs for guest seating lined the walls. There was a huge picture window, and, through the half-closed curtains, Katy could see it looked out over the gardens. Noticing the light from the TV, she wheeled over to see what was on. At first, she did not see the man slouched in the chair sleeping. When she did, she was slightly startled. He looked dead. She tried to turn her chair around to leave without being noticed, but she ran into another chair. And, the sound woke him. He looked up to see her, looking startled and wide-eyed. "Galina?" he asked.

"No, I'm not Galina. I'm Katy," she said in a hushed tone.

"What are you doing here?" he asked.

Katy thought, *That's the question of the day, isn't it?* but didn't say it aloud. She just said, "I was having trouble sleeping. It's my first night here. I'm sorry if I disturbed you."

"Katy? Katyusha? Ah yes . . . Ekaterina," he said with a Russian accent. "She was the greatest of the czarinas, you know?"

"Umm . . . no, I didn't know. Are you from Russia? What's your name?" She had not planned on a conversation with a strange Russian in the middle of the night.

"I am Dimitri Demidova," he said. "I have been placed in this prison by my daughter who thinks I am too old to care for myself." His voice rose as he spoke. "She—" his comment was cut short by an attendant entering the room.

"Dema, come on, buddy, you know you shouldn't be here at this time of night," he said.

As Dimitri reached for his cane, his demeanor quickly became ugly. Katy's mediator skills immediately kicked in, and she said, "Oh no, he heard me rolling around and came to see if he could help me. It's really my fault he's here."

Dimitri looked over at her suspiciously, and, then, he shot her a quick smile.

"Well, whatever the case, neither of you should be here. Let's get you both back to your rooms," the aide said as another aide appeared around the corner.

"Hey, Don, take the big guy here back to his room. I'll help the lady."

As Don helped Dimitri up, Dimitri gave Katy a high-five, which she returned. Katy actually smiled at the little diversion she had created. Returning to her room, she still could not sleep.

—

The next day, she looked for Dimitri in the great room but didn't see him. Harbor Place did not waste any time, and, immediately after breakfast, she was taken to physical therapy. About thirty minutes in, Katy wanted to go back to her room.

"OK, you guys, I've had enough for today. Maybe I'll come back again tomorrow?" Katy said.

"Well, actually, Ms. Glass, you're scheduled for an afternoon session today," the physical therapist said.

The physical therapist was empathetic, but it was very clear to Katy that her afternoon appointment was nonnegotiable.

Thinking quickly, Katy said, "Listen, I think my stump is showing signs of skin breakdown again. I really need to be careful."

The therapist looked over her stump but was not impressed. "I don't think it's anything to worry about. Now, can you please repeat what I just showed you a minimum of six times?"

Katy repeated the exercise and then tried again to feign her way out of PT. "You know, the area under my arms is sore from the crutches. I don't think I'm going to be able to work this afternoon."

"Don't worry, we won't be using your crutches today."

Finally, Katy exploded. "You fucking people have no idea what the hell you are doing. I'm telling you I can't do this shit, and I won't. Who the hell are you people anyway? I won't be back after lunch, you can be assured of that," she said, jaw clenched, one fist slamming the armrest of the wheelchair and her face screwed up tight with anger. With that, she dropped the weight in her hand on the floor and wheeled her chair out of the PT area.

Friggin' jerks, she thought. She wanted to return to her room but feared they would find her there too easily. She decided to try to hide in the garden. *I am a prisoner of war*, Katy thought to herself, *and these are my tormentors.*

It was a beautiful spring day inside the atrium, and life in the garden was beginning anew. Katy found a seat under the cherry blossom tree and looked up to see the beginnings of buds. Taking a deep breath, she almost felt relaxed, but her anguish clawed its way back to the forefront of her mind as she sat there. It was a constant struggle to stay on the other side of the sticky web of depression, a place of fog and darkness. It was also exhausting and slowly claiming more and more of her. She was so deep in her private hell that she didn't hear the footsteps as he approached her.

"Ekaterina! What are you thinking so hard about?" Dimitri asked.

She was so startled she almost fell out of her chair. "Oh, hello, Dimitri," she said, clutching her chest as she regained her composure. In the daylight, she was able to make out his salt-and-pepper hair, dark black eyes, and gray mustache. He seemed quite tall and lanky as he sat down on the bench beside her. He had on a nondescript black coat, black pants, and work boots. But, it was his smile that caught her attention. *He is a good-looking man for an old guy*, Katy thought. "How are you?" she asked, not really caring.

"Never better," he replied. "Unless you count the time that I was free to come and go as I pleased and live my life," he replied sarcastically, his voice escalating. "I can't believe I escaped Russia only to be entrapped here in this American institution!"

Katy looked at him. "What do you mean you escaped Russia?"

"Ekaterina, you are the great czarina, you know why we left Russia!" he replied.

"Dimitri, I'm Katy..."

He looked at her with surprise.

Ahh . . . so this is why you are here. You really are crazy, she thought to herself. "Dimitri," Katy said, thinking quickly, "let's go to the palace, find the horses, and we can leave this place."

Dimitri looked at her, hesitated for a second, then stood up and walked next to Katy as they went back to the great room. In the great room, Katy signaled to an aide who took Dimitri over to a corner and sat with him. Katy glanced back to see if he was OK and wheeled herself over to another table.

"Is he OK?" she asked one of the nurses.

"Dimitri? Oh yeah, he gets a little crazy sometimes. Usually a nap shakes him out of it."

"Umm . . . "

"Why, what did that old man tell you? He does this all the time to the new people, promising he will get them out of here. That old man is just wild with stories. Do you know he thinks he actually escaped from Russia at one time?"

"Did he?"

"Who knows, but not likely. He's as American as you and me, just has that Russian accent. It's cute, though, and he is certainly entertaining. He has a daughter who visits from time to time. Pretty girl, her name is . . . umm . . . Elena. That's it, Elena. Very nice woman, but he makes her life difficult with all of his running away. Anyway, don't believe half of what he tells you."

She then walked over to a table to stop a patient from taking another patient's snack away.

Oh wow, this place is a nut house, Katy thought. *How did I end up here?* Katy's misgivings about Harbor Place were interrupted by the appearance of one of the PT assistants. She began to protest, but, to Katy's surprise, instead of escorting her back to PT, he took her to a private office and told her to wait. Katy thought she was going to get a lecture from some administrative jerk about the hard time she had given the physical therapists. *Too damn bad. That's what they get paid for*, she thought as she stared out the window at the parking lot, trying to stir up her irritation in preparation for what she was sure would be an argument.

"Good afternoon, Katy, my name is Dr. Joseph Junger. I am one of the psychiatrists here at Harbor Place. I understand you're having some trouble adjusting to your surroundings and schedule." In the doorway stood a tall, balding, middle-aged man with thick glasses. He did not wear the traditional white coat, but his badge did verify he was, indeed, Dr. Junger.

Katy looked at him and snarled. "Doc, say what you need to, but don't expect me to do any talking. I don't need you or want anything to do with you," she said as she assessed him carefully.

"Really? OK, then do you mind if I take just a little bit of your time to share something I see over and over again with the vets who come through here? Maybe you can relate, maybe not. But, I would be interested in your opinion if you have one. Would that be OK?"

Katy was suspicious but thought that as long as she didn't have to say anything, this would be better than going to PT. "Why not? Just don't expect me to buy into the mumbo jumbo voodoo that you do," she replied.

"Oh, I like that . . . mumbo jumbo voodoo. I wonder what they will say to that at our next national conference. Hmm . . . I'll have to try that one out," he replied with a smile.

For the next hour, Dr. Junger described what he called an "interesting phenomenon."

"You know, humans as a species are quite resilient. I doubt we would have made it this far from our time as cavemen if we were not wired for survival with that instinct embedded in our very evolved brains. Human beings have rebounded from many man-made traumas, war, starvation, concentration camps, rape, nuclear fallout, bombs, murder, and natural disasters like floods, earthquakes, hurricanes, tornados, wildfires—you name it, as humans we've been through it all. What's interesting, Katy, is what I see when I look at people who have experienced 'trauma.' It seems as if their bodies hold the burden of what they have seen and been through. They walk around with clenched fists, slumped shoulders, gritted teeth, locked jaws . . . their bodies betray their psychic injuries, and most of them don't even realize it. A very special man named Bessel van der Kolk, another psychiatrist who studied trauma for many years, noticed this pattern in his trauma patients. He has diligently worked for a quarter of a century trying to unlock exactly what trauma does to people, and he's done some fascinating stuff. Here," he said, searching through a file cabinet. "I think I may have some pictures of some of his discoveries."

He stopped for a moment and looked through a couple of files before he pulled out two X-ray films and put them up on a view box.

"Katy, these are called functional MRIs. To explain it in the simplest of terms, they measure the activity in the brain when one thinks. In his research, Dr. van der Kolk found that certain areas of the brain, particularly those areas along the center of the brain . . . " He pointed to the scan, "shut down in the face of significant trauma. For instance, on this picture you can see that these midline structures are all lit up. The MRI was imaging this patient while he was doing breathing exercises and looking at tranquil pictures. But, look what happens when a script of his personal trauma is read to him. Those areas go dim, and some even disappear entirely," he said with some excitement. "This incredible finding has led the way to developing better techniques and treatment for those who have suffered trauma."

Katy's natural curiosity got the better of her, and, despite her initial vow to stay silent, she asked, "Why are these areas so important? Do we stop breathing or something?"

Encouraged, Dr. Junger continued. "No, Katy, but our breathing is altered. It's one of the symptoms that we see in people who have flashbacks. Do you know what I mean when I say flashback?"

Katy just glared at him.

"OK, well, what is even more interesting is that we find that people who have experienced trauma get stuck in the past, frozen in a place and time. Depression and a sense of futility set in because they can't make sense of the overwhelming sensations they experience. Trauma victims often detach from personal contact with others and withdraw into themselves for emotional safety. Because of this detachment, relationships become tricky. Some victims of trauma suffer immense shame for not being able to prevent the trauma. There are people who say they feel emotionally numb long after the occurrence. It's because trauma reorganizes our brains, and our perceptions of the world become skewed." He looked at Katy to see if she was still with him.

"Katy, did you know that trauma even affects our imagination? You might say 'so what,' but I would say imagination is the lifeblood of our lives. Without imagination, how would we ever solve problems? Without imagination, what would fuel our creativity? Without imagination, how do we envision a better life? We now know that trauma causes a reorganization of the way that we mentally handle our perceptions, and a lack of imagination plays a role in that. I have found Dr. van der Kolk's work incredibly informative, and it is the basis of my work. Interesting stuff, huh, Katy?"

Katy looked at him and thought, *OK, he's clearly another crazy person*. But, something he had said piqued her interest. Just as she was about to ask a question, he stood up and ended the session.

"Well, Katy, I have to go. I hope you have a good day," he said and left the room.

"Hey, Doc! Wait a minute. How am I supposed to get back to the great room?"

He shrugged his shoulders. "I guess the same way you got here, in your wheelchair." And, with that, he walked off.

Why, that rat bastard! Here I am in a wheelchair and he can't even take the time to push me back? What the hell? Katy thought. *What a jerk.*

—

Later, after finishing dinner, Katy returned to her spot under the cherry blossom tree. She was still processing her conversation with Dr. Junger and wanted some time to herself. But, there was Dimitri, sitting with his long legs crossed and leaning back against the bench.

"Hi, Dimitri," she said as she wheeled up to the bench. "How was your afternoon?"

"Ahh, Katyusha, so nice to see you again. I slept a little this afternoon and feel much better."

"Katyusha?" Katy asked. "What does that mean?"

"Your name is Katy, *da*?"

She smiled and nodded her head in agreement. "*Da*."

"In my country, we add this suffix to some of our names to indicate affection or to say we feel a softness toward another."

"So, would I say Dimitriusha?" Katy smiled at the sound of this.

Dimitri laughed. "No Katyusha, my 'nickname,' as you call it, is Dema. We have many different ways of saying names in Russia. It takes a little getting used to."

"I can see that."

"Katyusha, do you see this tree? Soon it will be dressed in pink. Just for you, the czarina."

"Oh, Dimitri, I don't know about that. It's going to be covered in blossoms whether I'm here or not."

Dimitri frowned at her. "Ekaterina, the simple pleasures of the garden should not be lost on someone so beautiful. My father taught me that the garden is the origin of life. What we sow is what we reap."

Katy looked at him with a skeptical eye. "Where did you develop such a philosophical personality?"

"Katyusha, have you ever been a prisoner?"

"Only in this place," she replied sarcastically.

Dimitri chuckled. "*Da*, I would agree. But there are worse prisons, where lives are lived out and discarded without remorse."

Katy frowned. She wasn't sure if he was serious.

"When I was thirteen or fourteen, I don't remember anymore, a member of Stalin's police force came to my house . . . " he started. And, for the next two hours, Dimitri told Katy the story of his imprisonment in the gulag.

When he finished, she could see that he was exhausted. She was speechless. "How did you live through that? Better still, how do you live with that now? It must have been horrifying, Dimitri. I can't even imagine."

With a sorrowful look on his face, Dimitri shook his head and said, "Unless you were there you can't fully know, it is impossible for me to convey with words the degree of brutality that men are capable of. It is impossible for me to describe how men function under such savagery and inhumanity."

"Dimitri, do the memories fade?" Katy asked meekly.

"No, Ekaterina, they lay in the back of my mind, fragmented and distorted. What brings them to life for me—flashbacks, I think you call them—is anybody's guess. Sometimes, when I hear a stern voice or someone yelling, these memories come rushing back to me out of nowhere. They rise like dragons in my mind, waiting to burn a hole in my soul."

Dimitri took a breath as he thought for a moment. "For instance, today I can tell you I am hungry, and you will understand. But sometimes my hunger takes me back to a different hunger, one I experienced in the camp. To try to describe what 'hungry' was in the prison camp . . . I have no words that allow you to comprehend the sucking agony that was hunger at that time. That period in my life is bereft of any recognizable description, and so are the memories," Dimitri said with a great sadness in his voice.

"Dimitri, how do you live with those . . . memories?" Katy asked, her face filled with concern.

"Ekaterina, I was lucky, my father's teachings kept me strong during that awful time. After my release, I found my wife, who reminded me there was still love and beauty in this world, and then my daughter came. For her I have lived, not without the pain of those memories but in spite of them. My wife and my daughter gave me new hope for a better life after my release.

They are the reason I have been able to continue. They are the reason I still live."

"Dimitri, we studied the Holocaust when I was in school, and I knew about Hitler's sick attempt to annihilate the Jews. But I don't remember anyone talking about the holocaust in Russia. Why isn't that in the history books?"

Sadly, Dimitri shook his head. "I don't know Katyusha. I don't know."

CHAPTER XII

The memory of trauma . . . acts like a foreign body . . .
like a splinter that causes an infection, it's the
body's response to the foreign object that becomes
the problem more than the object itself.

—BESSEL VAN DER KOLK

HARBOR PLACE
APRIL 2013

A month had passed since Katy's arrival at Harbor Place. She reluctantly continued daily PT and was forced to attend group therapy sessions, which seemed senseless to her, so she absolutely refused to participate. She was, however, starting to like Dr. Junger. He had a pretty good sense of humor and talked to her as if she were his student rather than his patient. He asked about her life before her deployment, and she proudly told him of her achievements in school and how she had come to be a member of the CST. She told him how she had thought she was going to be a war correspondent and how she found out her father had been one too. He asked what made her feel at peace with herself. She hung her head and said, "Working out."

He replied, "Dr. van der Kolk says, 'You can't be fully in charge of your life until you can acknowledge the reality of your body.'"

Katy's head snapped up. Glaring at him, she wordlessly wheeled her chair out of the office, making sure to slam the door as she left.

During another session, Dr Junger asked Katy if she knew why she was taking antidepressants.

She responded sarcastically, "Because I'm depressed. Come on, Doc, even I know that."

"Yes and no, Katy. Traumatized people have been found to have lower serotonin levels, which makes them hyperactive and compromises their ability to cope. Prozac, for instance, increases serotonin levels in the brain by preventing the reuptake of serotonin in the nerve endings. It provides a small measure of help for those feelings of rage and volatility. This type of medication can dampen the fear system and its fight-or-flight response."

Katy thought back on her behavior and the uncontrollable rage she'd felt with the physical therapists and nurses at Walter Reed.

"There is another thing that is interesting, Katy," he said as he put two brain scans up on the view box in his office. "Here, let me show you this. You see this area right here? This is Broca's area, the speech center in the brain. You see how you can barely see it on this scan? Well, there is a reason for that—we have found that people who have witnessed horrific events often lose access to Broca's area while they are experiencing the trauma. You've heard the expression, 'I was scared speechless.' Well, that's why. Blood flow is markedly decreased to this area during traumatic events. Those feelings of terror, rage, helplessness, and overwhelming fear can't be articulated because the brain cannot articulate that which it can't comprehend."

Katy thought back to Dimitri's comment—"no words to describe the hunger"—as she looked at the scans.

"Now, look at this area called Brodmann's area. It's lit up like a Christmas tree because this is where the brain registers images when they are first visualized. So, when words fail us, the brain resorts to flashbacks and nightmares as a way to sort things out, and it can readily retrieve those images. Does that make sense, Katy?"

Katy was intrigued and didn't want him to stop talking, but the session was over. "Why is it that just as you get interesting, the session ends?" Katy demanded as she turned to leave.

Dr. Junger shrugged his shoulders and smiled at her. "See you next time, Katy."

The next stop was PT. Katy still hated physical therapy. She felt like she was getting nowhere. It was also a cruel reminder of better days when she was the top physical specimen in her squad, when her future held great promise and excitement.

"Why do you insist that I try to do this? You already know I can't," Katy asked Rebecca, the physical therapist, as she once again attempted to convince Katy to use her prosthesis.

"Katy, every day is a new day. Try to focus on the fact that you are healing, even if it is only an inch at a time. One day, you will surprise yourself, I just know it," Rebecca said cheerfully.

"You call this healing?" Katy snapped. "I call this miserable goddamn torture. I would have been better off if the enemy had captured me. They would have at least killed me by now," she said, slamming her fist on the arm of her wheelchair. Her conversation with Dr. Junger flashed through her mind. *Whatever*, she thought, shaking her head, *Screw him*.

Katy continued to rebuff any attempts to try on her prosthesis and generally worked to make life difficult for everyone, including herself. She swore at the nurses as they checked her now well-healed stump, she kicked the aides out of her room whenever they came to help her, she sat insolently quiet in group, and she stayed in her darkened room as often as she could. The staff was patient and kept after her, but Katy was determined not to let anyone inside. Katy believed no one could understand her pain, except, perhaps, Dimitri.

After their conversation in the garden, the two had become fast friends and allies in the desert of Harbor Place. Both felt like prisoners of war being held against their will. Katy was impressed by Dimitri's intelligence, his Russian mystique, and the fact that he had survived unimaginable horrors. He had obviously been through a lot in his lifetime, and she took comfort in his presence. In fact, he was the *only* person in Harbor Place who made Katy feel safe enough to talk to.

After a particularly grueling day in PT, Katy went to the garden. She wheeled herself over to her favorite spot under the cherry blossom tree, now in full bloom, and allowed herself to cry in silence. She was so tired of trying, sick of being sick, and she was sure she would never walk again. As tears streamed down her face, she wiped her nose on the sleeve of her shirt.

"Ekaterina! Don't use your clothes. Here, use this," Dimitri said.

Katy jumped when she heard him. *Where did he come from? How does he always know when I'm here?* she thought. But she gratefully reached for the tissue. "Thank you, Dimitri." She sniffled.

"*Palshulsta.*[15] Now tell Dimitri why the beautiful czarina is shedding so many tears. You should be dancing and laughing, surrounded by many suitors," he said in his thick Russian accent.

Katy looked straight into his eyes and tried to hate him, but she couldn't. Instead, she said, "I think it's going to be a long time before I dance again, Dimitri. I don't know, I guess some days it's just easier to cry." She hesitated and then said, "Dimitri, can I tell you something?"

He nodded.

"I feel so angry! I feel like I've lost all control over my life. I shouldn't be here, the man I love died along with my best friend, and I can't find the strength to get out of my own way."

Dimitri looked at her and took her hand. "Your Excellency, your loss breaks my heart, but perhaps I can help you. Ekaterina, you are the greatest czarina ever in Mother Russia. You have more strength than you think."

Katy looked at the old man and wondered, *Is he for real?* But there was comfort in the feel of his hand on hers and in the tone of his voice.

"Do you remember when I told you how I was a prisoner for so many years?"

"Yes, of course. It's a horrible story, and I'm still amazed that you survived."

---

15   "You're welcome."

"Do you know why I survived, Katyusha?"

"You mentioned your father's teachings."

"You are correct. I survived because of my father. He was my greatest teacher. When I was young, we spent hours every day tilling the soil, bringing the dirt to life. He taught me that in order to eat, we had to work hard. We used a makeshift wooden plow, removed rocks from the soil to make it pliable for the plants, and we watched our hard work make the land come alive every year. But, he also taught me that sometimes it's not enough to just work hard and pray. Sometimes bad things happen, and you cannot avoid these things. Sometimes, like huge boulders in the garden, the ones you know you will never remove, you have to learn to work around them."

"But, Dimitri, they killed your father," Katy said with despair in her voice. She felt bad immediately after she said it.

"Ekaterina, I know. But my father's spirit lives on in me," he said. "Here and here." He pointed to his heart and head. "He taught me that life is nothing without dignity and hope, and no one can take that from you unless you give it away. His lessons allowed me to continue in the face of horrors that no one can imagine. He taught me that love is the only thing that can bring peace to a broken heart."

Katy's forehead wrinkled in concentration.

Very gently, Dimitri asked, "Your Highness, how did you lose your leg?"

Katy had put that story away, back into the recesses of her mind. It had been almost five months since she had been wounded. She was holding on to her story as if telling it would somehow make it all real. She desperately clung to the memories of the days when she felt whole and capable of taking on the world. Her memories of the past were so much better than her reality in the present. In her Army debriefing about the incident, she had given only the most salient details. She was also trying to keep Jack alive by holding on a little longer to their story. She feared talking about that night would be the end of everything that was Jack. But now, in the silence of the garden, surrounded by new blooms and flowering trees, Katy looked at Dimitri. Tentatively at first, she started to tell the story of that night.

"We were given information that a high-ranking al-Qaeda insurgent was hiding in a small village about twenty miles north of our base. He was our target, but the village he was hiding in was inhabited mostly by women and children. The men had fled or been captured. I was part of the Army Rangers Cultural Support Team. My sole purpose was to speak with the Afghani women so they weren't disgraced by speaking to our guys in uniform. It was a historical effort on the military's part to recognize and overcome the cultural barriers that were impeding our progress in the war. Of course, the MEDEVAC team was there. The man I loved was the flight surgeon for the team."

Katy turned her gaze away from Dimitri as she continued.

"That night, at 2330 hours we loaded onto the helicopter that took us to the village. Arriving exactly at midnight, the Army Rangers exited the helicopter first, as was protocol, and my partner and I waited for the all clear signal from them. We were connected by headsets, so I could hear everything that was happening. My captain gave the all clear, and my partner and I went to where the women were gathered with their children. We were a great team, Shveta and I. I can't speak Pashto, but she could. And, between the two of us, we were really good at our jobs," she said with a sigh. "We had not even started talking with the women when I heard the crack of gunfire. There was no order from the captain to retreat, so we continued moving forward, knowing the boys would take care of business. Unfortunately, someone, I still don't know who, stepped on a daisy chain."

Dimitri looked puzzled.

"A daisy chain IED is a land mine that arms multiple other land mines in the vicinity once it's set off. All hell broke loose once that happened. My captain yelled, 'We are under attack!' and just as he said that, he was blown to bits. Shveta and I tried to get as many women and children as we could to go with us, but they were scared and started running in the opposite direction of the helicopter. I should have understood then that they had been told the direction of safety, but it didn't dawn on me until it was too late. I just knew I had to get them and Shveta back to the helicopter. Shveta had already made an about-face and was running toward the helicopter. I saw her running, and in the chaos something clicked. I realized she was running into a minefield. I started to scream at her to stop, but it was too late—I watched my best friend get blown to pieces. She was my best friend in Afghanistan. We did everything together," Katy said, with tears streaming and the horror of that night written across her face.

"My friend, the flight surgeon on the MEDEVAC, saw me start to move. He jumped from the helicopter and started running toward me. It was at that moment I realized the same thing was going to happen to me if I didn't stop running—so I did—but he did not. I saw him fly through the air like a rag doll. I dropped down and body crawled to him thinking I could save him.

"I remember cradling him in my arms and sobbing. 'Oh, Jack, what have you done?' The smell of burning flesh made me vomit violently. Out of the dust and pandemonium, a young guy, one of the medics grabbed my arm and screamed at me 'Ma'am, we're out of here, now!' But, I don't think I really heard him. All

I remember are the sounds of explosions and how much they hurt my ears.

"I do remember looking up at him, because he had a death grip on my arm. I was so dazed and confused, but I allowed him to remove my arm from around Jack. In seconds, we were up and running zig-zag patterns over the rough terrain, trying to dodge enemy fire and praying we would avoid any other pressure plates that would set off more devastation. Another IED exploded behind me. That shock wave propelled me face-first to the ground. I had sweat stinging my eyes, and I tasted blood from a split lip. I was stunned by the explosion's force, and thought, *That was really friggin' close*. It couldn't have been a millisecond later when I felt the pain in the back of my leg and wetness running down my pant leg. Crazy that it didn't dawn on me that I was hurt. My mind was still on Jack and Shveta.

"The medic who had helped me was now lying on the ground just behind me, not moving. Another medic from the helicopter moved quickly and picked me up off the ground. Somehow, we made it back to the helicopter. He literally threw me into the helicopter bay, where the guys grabbed me, pushed me onto a stretcher, and began tending to my bleeding leg.

"'Kandahar, we are lifting off, have eight wounded and multiple casualties. We're gonna have to come back to collect the dead.' I remember hearing that through my headset.

"Over the helicopter's screaming rotors, the medic yelled at me, 'Hang in there, Second Lieutenant. It's going to be a rough ride.' And, he took off my headset.

"I can't even begin to tell you how frightening the helicopter ride was out of there. The craft shook from the concussions of IEDs exploding and mortar fire erupting. Bullets pinged off the side of the craft as we made our way into the air. Thank God the desert dust offered some coverage as we went dark trying to fly without attracting any large mortar shells.

"The weather that night had been very temperate, but I couldn't stop shivering. After the IV was started, they gave me morphine, and the rest of the trip is a foggy memory. I do remember the date though. It was Sunday, January 1, 2013, New Year's Day. A time of celebration for most people but not in Kandahar, Afghanistan. Not that night. All I kept thinking over and over was, *Why?*"

"Why?" Dimitri asked.

"Why didn't he stop? I'm sure he saw that I had stopped moving. Why did he keep coming? Why did he always have to be the first one to run into danger? He was like that, you know? Always the first to volunteer for anything perilous. He *never* let the MEDEVAC go out on a risky mission without him on board. Extra duty at the hospital—that was Jack." Katy felt the lump in her throat cutting off her words.

Finally, she said, "Dimitri, I killed them all," and hid her face in her hands as she broke down into sobs.

Dimitri placed his hand on her knee and let her cry for a few minutes. He then offered her another tissue as he took both of her hands. "Ekaterina, that is an awful burden to carry. Feeling responsible for getting someone killed. That pain . . ." He trailed off. "Ekaterina, there is a rule. Where there is war, people die. You cannot change that. Your friends were casualties of war. Your soldier friend chose to serve you in your time of need. This was his decision. He obviously cared about you—enough to give his life. Now you dishonor his memory."

Katy looked up at Dimitri, surprised by the admonition and angry.

"Yes, I see the anger in your eyes, but listen to me. He gave his life for you, but now you want to take this moment away from him. You want to carry the burden of his death as if it's yours to carry. Did you want to be the hero, Ekaterina? Your flight surgeon will be recognized for his sacrifice to protect you. Honor his life and death by allowing him his decision. Otherwise, you dishonor his memory by your selfish desire to keep him alive." Then, very softly, he said, "You have to let go, Katyusha, because this thing that happened . . . you cannot change it."

Katy sobbed even harder as Dimitri's words settled into her consciousness. She had been holding on so tightly, trying so hard to change the fact that Jack was dead.

"Dimitri, I'm so angry and so sad. How do I let go? My heart hurts so much, sometimes I can barely breathe," she asked, choking on her tears.

"Ahh, Your Highness, only time can heal that wound," he said, very gently. "In the meantime, you must find the strength to let go of your bitterness. It only weakens your spirit and holds you back. But, if you feel weak, you come to Dimitri, and I will hold your hand."

She looked at him and saw the deepest compassion in his eyes. Through her tears, she gave him a weak smile. "I think maybe we have a lot in common, Dimitri."

"Yes, my dear Katyusha, I think you are right." That day, Dimitri was there for his precious czarina.

—

Two days later, Katy wheeled into Dr. Junger's office and said without hesitation, "Doc, today it's my turn to talk."

He replied, nodding in agreement, "OK, Katy, come on in. I've been waiting for this moment."

For the next hour, Katy told the story of the failed mission and what had happened on that fateful night.

CHAPTER XIII

People are so afraid to let go—afraid of
falling and other dire consequences.
But what if when you let go, you were to fly instead?

—C. M. SCHAFFER

Katy's days continued at a monotonous pace. Each day started
with breakfast in the great room at seven o'clock. This meant
she was up at six-thirty every morning, except on the weekends,
when breakfast was served at eight. At breakfast, Katy sat with
Dimitri to see how he was doing each morning. She had become
quite fond of Dimitri, and she secretly kept an eye out for him
as he went through his daily routine. She made sure they had
breakfast together each morning, and he'd make her laugh at
some obscure insight he shared with her. After breakfast, on her
way to PT, she stopped in the great room to see what he was

doing. Usually, he was in the gardens with a book. *He is such a voracious reader*, Katy thought.

There had been a subtle shift in Katy's attitude, and her mother even noticed it during a phone conversation.

"Hello, Katy, darling. How are you doing?"

"Hi, Mom, I'm OK today. Today is a pretty good day."

"Why is that, honey?" her mother asked, hesitantly. She never knew what Katy was going to say, and the harsh words that comprised Katy's recent vocabulary weighed heavily on her mother.

"Well, for one thing, the garden is starting to look gorgeous from my window. Today the sun is shining. I may go out and sit in it for a while."

Her mother wondered for a brief second who was on the other end of the phone, but said, "Honey, I'm so happy you want to go outside. It's been a long time since you enjoyed the outdoors."

"I know, Momma, but . . . I think today will be different." They went on to talk about a few other things. At the end of the conversation, Katy offered, "Mom, I'm so sorry for what I have put you and Daddy through. But, I'm getting there." Katy heard her mother trying to choke back tears as they said their goodbyes. "I'll talk to you soon, Mom. Tell Daddy I love him."

Katy's progress in her sessions with Dr. Junger seemed to move at a glacial pace. Their latest effort was learning breathing techniques to help Katy get past her panic attacks and sudden surges of rage. Dr. Junger explained, "Katy, paying attention to our breath is one of the ways we can directly train our arousal system to chill out when we are in a state of high anxiety. It's an ancient technique used by Eastern medicine for thousands of years. In this country, we've been slow to pick it up, quite frankly, because Western medicine is too egotistical and Cartesian-oriented to think that 'ancient Chinese medicine' might actually work. But, that's neither here nor there. There are physiological reasons why this works. When you take slow, deliberate breaths, it's like putting on the brakes for your nervous system. Whenever you have emotional triggers, you have to focus on your breathing. Sounds simple, doesn't it? But it really does require some training and practice because it's not as easy as it sounds."

"So, when I'm about to go bonkers on the PT staff, I can stop myself if I think about breathing?" Katy asked, disbelief written all over her face.

"Not exactly. You can't just think about your breathing, you have to practice breathing regulation. Let me show you. Take a deep breath." Katy complied. "Now, as I count to ten, slowly let it out. One, two, three . . . " Katy tried to mimic Dr. Junger's breathing. "And, finally, ten."

"Umm, I don't think I can hold my breath that long, Doc."

"Don't hold your breath, Katy, let it out very slowly. Let's try again." The rest of the session was devoted to breathing exercises.

In another session, Dr. Junger introduced Katy to Eye Movement Desensitization and Reprocessing. As Katy repeated the story of that horrible night in Kandahar, Dr. Junger asked her to follow his index finger as he moved it slowly back and forth about twelve inches away from her eyes. Within seconds, the horror, rage, and incomprehensible memories of her experience in Kandahar flooded over Katy. She could feel herself being splattered with Shveta's body parts, and she could hear the thud of Jack's body hitting the ground as clearly as if she was there again. She could hear the mortars firing and bullets flying by her head. She felt herself crawling toward Jack to get to his dead body.

Dr. Junger kept offering encouraging sounds and asked her to pay attention to what she was feeling.

"I feel like I'm going to vomit, Dr. Junger," Katy said.

"It's OK, Katy, I'm here with you. Just follow my finger and tell me what you are seeing and feeling."

"Oh my God! Shveta!"

"You're OK, Katy. I'm right here."

"No, no, no, no," Katy moaned.

"What do you see, Katy?"

"The young medic who grabbed me and made me start for the helicopter, they just killed him too. He didn't deserve to die. He was just trying to help me," Katy said, suddenly sobbing.

"You're right, Katy, he didn't deserve to die. Keep following my finger. You're doing OK."

"Ow! Goddamn, that hurt!" Katy said reaching for the back of her leg. "Why is my pant leg so wet? They're throwing me onto the helicopter so fast. I don't think I was even on a stretcher before we started to take off … Doc, I can't … "

"OK, Katy, good job," he said, dropping his finger. "I know that the first time can be really intense and pretty frightening. But, tell me, how do you feel right now?"

"Well … I don't know. I'm surprised that exercise didn't send me into a flashback—that's what usually happens, you know. In fact, now that we're done, those memories don't seem as intense. Is that weird?"

"No, Katy, that's exactly what is supposed to happen. EMDR loosens up the mind's ability to access memories and images from the past and, for some reason, although we don't know exactly why, lessens the intense emotions surrounding those memories. It allows you the opportunity to observe your experience from a different perspective. Would you be willing to give it another go in our next session?"

"Sure, Doc, but I think right now I need a nap."

"Good, that means you've released a large amount of tension that you have been carrying around in your body. You did good today, Katy. I'm impressed."

Katy left the office, feeling strangely relieved.

Katy's dread of PT was abating as well. She was much less critical of the staff and had fewer meltdowns. The tissue around her amputation site was healed and seemed much less sensitive these days. She could bear weight on her prosthesis without pain. Now, it was just a matter of finding her balance again, but she was having difficulty regaining stability. She tried, but, if it weren't for her "handlers," she would definitely fall.

One day at breakfast she confided in Dimitri. "Dimitri, I am trying, really I am, but I just can't seem to find my balance on this new leg. I feel like my upper body is just not lining up over my legs, and I fall."

Dimitri thought for a moment and then said, "Ekaterina, Dimitri may have a plan. I will get back to you."

Katy just smiled at him and said, "*Spaciba*, Dimitri." She never guessed that, several days later, he would come to her with his fully formed plan.

Letters of Forgiveness

Katy was sitting under the cherry blossom tree after a long, difficult PT session when she saw Dimitri coming toward her, accompanied by a very petite woman. As they came closer, Katy thought, *Wow, she's really pretty. Where did Dimitri find her?*

The woman with Dimitri had long auburn hair pulled into a ponytail that swung back and forth as she walked. She appeared to be in her early forties, with high cheekbones, an angular jaw, and beautiful green eyes. Her muscular, yet lithe, build was displayed under a leotard and Lycra workout pants. There did not appear to be an ounce of fat on her. Her smile, which exposed a set of gorgeous teeth, was bright as day. Katy thought, *This woman is charged with energy.*

"Ekaterina, I thought you would be here," Dimitri said. "I want you to meet my favorite daughter, Elena. Elena, this is Ekaterina."

"Oh, Papa, stop. I am your only daughter," Elena said as she smiled and reached out to shake Katy's hand.

"Oh, you're Elena. Hi, my name is Katy. Dimitri talks about you all the time. You're the dancer."

"That is why I wanted you to meet Elena. She is a dancer. She can help you find your balance again. I have already talked to her about your problem, and she has agreed to try to help."

"Oh, Dimitri! That's so kind of you, but I couldn't impose on Elena like that. I'm sure she has many other things to do besides taking care of a broken soldier."

Elena stepped in. "Katy, if it were any other person, I would say no. But my father talks about you all the time. I think you have been good for him, and I appreciate that. Besides, my husband was a soldier too."

"Was?"

"He was killed in the Middle East."

"Oh my, I'm so sorry. Dimitri did not share that with me."

"Don't worry," Elena said. "It would be my privilege to help you if I can. I will be honest. I have no training in this type of work. I only know what I can teach you as a dancer."

"Elena," Katy started to say.

"Please, Katy, everyone calls me Lena."

"OK, Lena, if you are willing, I am ready to do anything that is different from what I have been doing here. To be honest, the people here are very good, but the monotony is starting to get to me, and I'm losing focus again."

"So, it's settled. Shall I pick you up tomorrow?" Elena asked.

"Tomorrow? So quickly? Umm ... OK, sure, why not?" Katy shrugged her shoulders.

"Papa, be good, I will say hello tomorrow when I pick up Katyusha," she said as she turned to walk away.

Dimitri said something to her in Russian that Katy didn't understand, but it made Elena turn around and kiss him on the cheek before she left. Katy smiled. The exchange reminded her of her own father.

The next day, Elena arrived as promised. She said a brief hello to Dimitri and, then, wheeled Katy out to the car. Once Katy was in the car, they were off to the studio.

"Wow, Lena. You folded that wheelchair up like a pro."

"My father has been in a wheelchair in the past. I learned how to manage it."

"Oh, I didn't know that about him."

"I suspect there are many things you don't know about him," Lena said.

The drive to the studio was very short. Once they arrived, Lena wheeled Katy in and asked her to put her prosthesis on.

"I would like to see how you move before we start."

"OK. Do you have something I can hang on to, because I'm pretty wobbly?" Katy said, feeling a bit intimidated.

"Yes, we can use the barre on the wall over there."

Once she was against the barre, Katy stood. As she predicted, she was very unsteady and needed the barre to keep from falling.

"Hmm . . . try lifting your hip on the other side, like this," Lena said, demonstrating what she wanted.

Katy tried, and there was an immediate difference in how her weight was distributed. "I feel a difference, but I'm not sure it helps the wobbles."

"OK, don't worry, Katy. I didn't expect to fix the problem in the first five minutes," Lena said, smiling as she reached over to shift Katy's weight to her good leg. "Try to feel how this changes your vertical center."

"My what?" Katy asked.

"Oh, of course, some terminology lessons first, eh, Katy? OK. We talk about the imaginary lines that run through our bodies that connect us to the floor and to gravity as our vertical center. I always like to tell my students that, while they dance with a partner, their most important partner is the floor. That is where balance and coordination begin. The other important concept you need to know about is counterbalance. When I dance with my partner, I move across my center to the 'almost' point. What I mean by that is I move across my center to a point that almost takes me off my leg, but because I am using my partner for counterbalance, I don't fall. Let's start with those ideas and see where they take us. How does that sound?"

"This is your territory, Lena. I am in your hands."

They spent the next hour talking about concepts of balance and how gravity and the floor play an equal part in movement. Katy was impressed with Elena's knowledge of anatomy and physics. Explanations like these were lacking in her PT sessions at Harbor Place. Some of the things Elena told her actually made sense. At the end of their session, Katy was ready to return for more.

"When can we do this again, Lena?"

"When do you want to come back? I can schedule you as one of my lessons whenever you like."

"How about the day after tomorrow? That will give me time to process what we've talked about today. At least then it will be in my head. I'm not sure how long it will take to get it into my body," Katy said with a big grin.

"That is the trick, Katy. Feeding our knowledge to our muscles takes time. But, Papa says you are smart and a hard worker. That will help. We'll plan on the day after tomorrow at the same time."

Elena dropped Katy back off at Harbor Place and, once in her room, Katy suddenly felt exhausted. *That took more out of me than I thought. Maybe there is hope for me*, she thought as she lay down on her bed. She fell into a deep sleep until dinner time.

—

In her next session with Dr. Junger, Katy told him about Elena and what they were doing. Junger was enthusiastic about her participation in movement exercise. "Katy, do you remember in one of our first sessions when I asked you what made you feel alive, and you said, 'Working out'?"

"Yes, and I remember I stormed out of that session," Katy said,

Dismissing the memory, he said, "No worries, Katy. There is a reason that working out makes you feel so good."

"Endorphins?"

"Well, that plays a role in it, but it's deeper. Have you noticed that when you are having a flashback, or you encounter a trigger of some sort, your body tenses? You may sweat or tremble, but your body always reacts in some way."

"No, I haven't really noticed. All I know is I am consumed by fear and gut-wrenching sickness. Several times, I've felt like I had ants crawling all over me."

"OK. Exactly!" he said, quickly standing up from his desk. "Gut-wrenching sickness is exactly the type of symptom I am talking about. Movement therapy, yoga, and qigong all seem to help trauma patients reintegrate their body sensations with their feelings. I believe movement therapy can help regulate the nervous system, which in turn regulates our internal responses to stress. You must know people who complain of chronic neck pain, migraines, or back pain, and no one can find anything anatomically wrong. They should probably be checking out the brain's anatomy. That's where somatic complaints live. If you can develop a more sensitive attitude toward your body and its sensations, you can learn to look inward and hear what your body is telling you. The concepts Lena is asking you to learn, muscle isolation and finding your center of gravity—these are the precepts of mind-body awareness in trauma. Identifying your muscles and being able to isolate them has deep implications for creating a more mindful approach to the feelings and bodily sensations you experience when you are having a flashback."

"Wow, who would have thought," she said. "I guess we'll see, won't we?"

Dr. Junger just smiled in agreement.

—

The next several weeks were a whirlwind of physical therapy, sessions with Dr. Junger, and lessons with Elena. Katy loved being in the studio with Elena. The studio's energy reflected Elena— electric, spirited, and full of life. Unlike physical therapy, which was repetitive and boring, the studio was a place full of promise, the smell of hard work, and something new every day. Memories of what it took to accomplish physical feats were dredged up by her time in the studio, and it brought back an old mindset for Katy. Acknowledging that her lack of progress in PT was partly related to her attitude, she was slowly rediscovering the attitude she'd had before her injury. The studio had a life of its own, and, more importantly, Katy felt like she belonged in this community of people. At first, the little girls were very curious about her prosthetic leg, and she was not sure how to handle it.

But, Elena suggested, "Just let them see it and touch it. Then, they'd forget about it." She had been right. By the third week of lessons, both the students and the parents had brought her and her prosthesis into the fold.

Katy looked forward to her lessons with the "crazy Russian lady," as she fondly referred to Elena. They actually had a lot in common. Both were organizers, planners, and hard workers, and they enjoyed the stimulation of physical activity. Katy liked that Lena ran a tight ship. It was reminiscent of her days at Fort Bragg. Lena's students were always on time, well prepared, and very respectful, and so were the teachers. Katy also liked Andrei, who she thought was cute and so attentive to Elena. She wondered why he and Elena weren't together. One day, she asked Elena about Andrei.

"Lena, how long have you known Andrei?"

A big smile broke out on her face as she said, "Andrei has been a part of my life since I moved here from Russia. We have known each other since I was sixteen years old." Looking over her shoulder at him, she continued. "I don't know what I would have done without him in my life. He has been with me through all of my ups and downs. He really is one of the good guys in this world."

"I can see that he is very devoted to you, the studio, and the students."

"Yes, thank God he's here. I'm not sure I would have survived Jack's death without him to lean on."

A gut-wrenching chill ran through Katy. "Jack?" she asked. "Wa . . . wa . . . was that your husband's name?" she stuttered.

"Yes. Now, Katy, today I want you to try to walk down the barre with your prosthesis. Do it slowly and think about each thing we have worked on for the last few weeks. I think you're ready."

Katy, with some effort, put this coincidence out of her mind. She trusted Lena's judgment and reached for the barre to pull herself up. Thinking very hard about the things they had practiced, Katy tried to apply each one as she took her first step. She looked up in surprise and said, "Hey, Lena, look, I'm still standing."

"Well, of course you are. Now, take another step."

The next step was more difficult because it was on her prosthetic leg. Katy took a deep breath and counted to three. *Here we go*, she thought. She could feel herself shifting her weight, lifting her hip the way Lena had taught her, using her leg for balance, and *voila*! She took a step with her prosthetic leg. Tears ran down her cheeks as she turned to Elena and said, "OK, Lena, now can you teach me how to dance, too?"

Elena smiled at her and gave her a hug. "Anything is possible, Katy. You just have to learn how to make it happen."

"Let me try one more combination," Katy said with more determination than she had felt in a very long time.

"Do it," Elena said.

Katy took the first step again on her good leg. By this time, everyone in the studio had stopped what they were doing to watch. They all knew her story, and everyone in the studio was genuinely interested in seeing her achieve her goal. When she took her second step, the group broke out in huge applause, whoops, and hollers. Everyone came over to congratulate a very tearful, but happy, Katy.

CHAPTER XIV

Blame has never once enhanced healing.

—CAROLYN MYSS

The letter from Kandahar arrived on a Tuesday. Katy found it sitting on top of her bureau when she came back from a morning group session. A sudden jolt of adrenaline rushed through her, and, for a moment, she was paralyzed, flooded with memories of Kandahar. Using the techniques that Dr. Junger had taught her, she slowed her breathing. Inside the envelope, she found a note from a friend of hers back in Kandahar wishing her a speedy recovery. *All that anxiety over a get-well card. Really, Katy?* she thought. As she replaced the card in the envelope, she noticed another envelope inside it.

"What's this?" she said aloud.

She pulled out the second envelope. The note clipped to the sealed envelope just said, "They found this in Jack's personal effects. It's addressed to you."

Oh my God! she thought. Her heart was racing a hundred miles an hour as she looked at the envelope in disbelief. Six months had gone by since she last talked to Jack. Her hands shook as she stared at the envelope. Part of her wanted to rip it open and inhale whatever it was he had left her, to feel his presence one more time, to have him with her if only in spirit. But she also felt an inexplicable trepidation, as if what she held in her hand was another bomb ready to go off.

Elena's revelation that her husband's name was Jack had unnerved Katy and started a slow but steady new cascade of jitters and anxiety. Even Dr. Junger had commented on her heightened state of arousal. Katy brushed it off as nothing, but she had a sick feeling deep inside. Since Elena used her maiden name, Katy was not sure if she was being overly paranoid or not. She thought about asking Dimitri but couldn't bring herself to do it. Besides, Dimitri had been really confused recently, and she was a little worried about him.

Twenty minutes went by, and she still had not opened the envelope. *What is wrong with me? This is from Jack. Open the damn envelope!* Just as she was about to open it, an orderly knocked on her door to collect her for physical therapy. She put the letter in the drawer of her bedside table. *Later*, she thought, a little relieved.

—

When Katy finally returned to her room that evening, she reluctantly opened the bedside drawer and pulled out the envelope. *Dimitri is right. I should honor Jack's sacrifice and let go of the burden of his death.* Sitting on the edge of her bed, she carefully opened the precious envelope. Inside was a letter written on Jack's official Army stationary. *Just like Jack to write me a letter using Army stationary*, she thought to herself with a little chuckle.

She opened the tri-folded piece of paper and began to read,

Dear Katy,

Precious Katy, if you are reading this then I am dead. I want you to know that having you here in Kandahar has made the unbearable bearable. I hope you will make it home safely and think back on our time together with great fondness. I also hope you will understand why I am going to ask for your discretion. Believe me, I was going to tell you this, but the time never seemed right. I am married. I have a wife and two kids. Obviously, I have not been much of a husband, and certainly not a good father, but I really don't want them to find out about us. It would not serve any purpose, and it would just open wounds that, at this point, are better left covered. Let's just chalk up our affair as another casualty of war. I hope you can find it in your heart to forgive me. We had a good time, kid.

Stay safe and go home alive,

Jack

Married!? Married? I would never have guessed it in a million years. No pictures, no talk of her, nothing. Maybe I should have known. He was always listening to that song about the lonely war wife. Forgive him?! Does he really think I can forgive that? After this? After the amount of mental anguish and pain that I have spent on him? How could I have fallen for this guy? How could I have been so stupid? What the hell, Jack! Why didn't you tell me?! She caught a glimpse of herself in front of her mirror and, in her rage, picked up a glass figurine and threw it at her image as tears streamed down her face. *I thought we were in love. Oh, Jack, I really loved you. You must have thought I was an easy mark, too simple and naïve to catch on to your games. I wonder how many other women you played. I have suffered so much because of—*

"You!" she screamed. "How could you do this . . . I believed you. You are a liar! Nothing but a liar . . . a liar," she cried, collapsing onto her bed. "I was just starting to believe again! Oh my God, Jack, how . . . how can you just take that away from me?" she sobbed into her pillow. "How could you do this to me?"

Katy cried herself to sleep, and, for the first time in several weeks, she had nightmares of death, deceit, and deception.

CHAPTER XV

Friendship is a single soul dwelling in two bodies.
—ARISTOTLE

"I will pick you both up at one o'clock on Sunday," Elena said as she stood up and bent over to kiss her father on the cheek. "Be well, Papa. I'll see you soon." She turned to walk toward the door, giving Katy a wave, and left.

"So, Ekaterina, we will have an outing with my daughter and her twins. I'm not sure if any of your military training will have prepared you adequately for those two," he said, smiling. Katy could see he was looking forward to the day.

Glad for the opportunity to get out of Harbor Place, Katy pushed her discomfort aside. Ever since reading Jack's letter she had been distracted by her conflicted feelings and increasing flashbacks. Feeling betrayed, hurt, and crazy, Katy was retreating back into her shell. Her attention span was limited, her lack of concentration was making her impatient again, and the PT staff was feeling the brunt of it.

She kept telling herself that their relationship would never have happened if she knew he was married. *Maybe that's why he didn't tell me. He knew*, she thought. *But, he sacrificed himself that night to protect me. You don't do that unless you're in love, right?* She sighed. Her bigger worry was Elena. What if Jack really was her husband? Deep down, Katy already knew the answer. She would have to talk to Dimitri and solidify the truth. She wasn't sure what she would do with the truth, but she had to know.

For some inexplicable reason, lunch on Sunday was moved from Elena's house to the local Denny's instead. Katy looked on in amazement as Dimitri came to life with Elena's twins. He laughed and giggled as much as they did. Conversation around the table was easy and mostly focused on how quickly the twins were growing and their recent accomplishment of learning how to climb out of their cribs. "I think it may be time for big boy and big girl beds," Elena said. The twins both giggled and said "Yay!" in unison. The food was simple but delicious. They all ate huge portions, and, when they left, they were stuffed.

From there, Elena took them to the park, so the kids, including Dimitri, could play.

Katy watched Dimitri looking as spry as a teenager as he played with the twins. Never in a million years would she have believed he was a nursing home patient. He pushed the twins on the swings, sat on the teeter-totter with them, rode the carousel over and over again, and laughed and laughed. Katy smiled at the "three children."

"Look at him, Lena, he's so alive out there. I don't think I've ever seen him with this much energy. He obviously loves those kids."

"Yes, and Sasha and Tasha love their *dedushka*," Lena said, looking up at the sky, eyes closed, soaking in the sun as they sat on a picnic bench.

"Sasha and Tasha, those are not nicknames you hear in this country. What are the twins' real names, Lena?" Katy asked.

"We call Alexander, Sasha, and Natalia is Tasha."

"I like those names. I really can't get over how fast they're growing. I think I saw them about two weeks ago at the studio, and they look like they've grown a foot," Katy said.

"I know. I can't keep them in clothes or shoes. They're outgrowing everything so quickly. I wonder what their father would think if he could see them now. You know, he wasn't home when they were born. Thank God Andrei was there. In fact, he wasn't home for most of the time we were married. Papa was angry when we got married. He thought we rushed into it, and he was really upset when we eloped. Turns out he was right, I guess. I never saw much of Jack after we were married."

Katy's heart was racing. She felt like it was going to jump right out of her chest. *No, no, it's just a coincidence. There are a million Jack's in the world*, she tried to convince herself. Katy said nothing and let Elena go on.

"Papa, not so high," Elena yelled at Dimitri as he pushed the twins on the swings. "Papa wasn't the best father, but he has been a wonderful *dedushka* . . . you would say grandfather."

"Lena, he is a good man. I am so sorry for what is happening to him."

"Yes, dementia is a brutal kidnapper. Did you know my father was a writer back in Russia?"

"Yes, he mentioned he used to write a long time ago."

"It's what forced our escape from Russia. Him and his reckless writing."

"Reckless?"

"Well, maybe not reckless, but Papa was a dissident and, as a little girl, I just always thought it caused us a lot of trouble. What I remember as a child is my parents constantly arguing over his writing. My mother would accuse him of setting us up for trouble."

"Wow, that must have been very difficult to understand as a young girl."

"Yes, and, when we escaped Russia, he apparently forgot to bring something with him," she said with an edge to her voice.

"What was that?" Katy asked

"My mother," Elena said sarcastically.

"Oh, wow, Lena, do you really think he purposefully left your mother behind? You know, when he is having a delusional moment, all he does is talk about her. He asks for her constantly when he's confused. I'm actually surprised to hear you say that."

"Don't be fooled by him. He asks only from a guilty conscience." At that moment, Sasha fell, skinned his knee, and started to wail.

When everything settled down, Elena said, "OK, I think we have all had enough of a good time. It's time to go. Besides, I promised I would have you both back by four this afternoon, and it's almost four." While the twins loudly protested the departure, they loaded up the car. Dimitri consoled Sasha, still hurting some, while Elena drove, and Tasha fell asleep against his arm. Pulling into Harbor Place's circular driveway, Katy looked back at Dimitri. *I've never seen him so peaceful,* she thought. Elena unloaded Katy's wheelchair, and Dimitri took great care helping her transfer from the car. After multiple hugs and kisses for the twins from Dimitri, Elena herded the kids back into the car.

"Thank you so much for asking me to come along, Lena. I had a nice day." Katy smiled.

"Yes, I'm glad you came. It was nice having you along. We'll do it again." Elena smiled back at Katy. "I'll see you at the studio. I have a few new things I want to try with you."

Dimitri stood behind Katy's wheelchair as they drove away, then wheeled her back into Harbor Place. The knot in Katy's stomach was growing.

CHAPTER XVI

From caring comes courage.

—LAO TZU

The day was bright with sunshine, and birds were singing expectantly. It was the kind of day that made you want to sit outside and soak in the possibilities of new beginnings. Katy was feeling good about the increased time she was spending walking with her prosthesis. That afternoon, Dimitri and Katy walked out together after lunch to sit under the cherry blossom tree, which was still in full bloom. The scent of cherry blossoms, hyacinths, and lilies of the valley filled the air. It was intoxicatingly sweet and a pleasure to the senses. The garden was alive and vibrant, and the sound of the waterfall filled the atrium.

"Wow, Dimitri, look at this place. It's magnificent. I can't believe how long the blossoms have lasted on this tree."

"*Da*, Katyusha, this is a beautiful time to be alive," he said as they settled under the cherry blossom tree. The stream seemed to babble with a sweet song of promise.

"Dimitri, I need to ask you something—actually, two things. They're kind of personal, and I'll understand if you don't want to answer them."

"What would you like to know, Katy?" he asked with fatherly concern.

Katy knew she had his full attention whenever he called her by her American name.

"Elena told me that you 'forgot' to bring her mother with you when you left Russia. She seems so angry about it. I told her I didn't believe that you purposefully left her behind because, when I hear you talk of her, it is with great love and devotion."

Dimitri's face became very solemn, and Katy thought she saw tears well up in his eyes.

"Katy, after my release from the gulag I returned to Moscow."

Katy nodded in acknowledgment.

"It was a most difficult transition—a slave for ten years and then suddenly a free man. But, somehow, I found work in what you would call a grocery store. After several years there, I met the most beautiful woman I had ever seen. I still remember the date, May 22, 1956. I was twenty-seven, and she was nineteen. She came in almost daily to buy fruits and vegetables. We would talk, and time would stand still. I fell in love with her almost immediately. We were married five years later. My Galina was not only beautiful but kind and a very talented ballerina. Lena gets her talent from her mother," he said with obvious pride. "Galina also understood my writing. She knew I needed to tell my story. But, she had to be very careful as she was the darling of the politburo. She could not be the Bolshoi's prima ballerina and stand up against Communism at the same time.

"For a while, we made it work. I loved her and would have given my life for her. When she had Elena, seven years later, I thought that perhaps her time with the ballet was over. But, shortly after Lena's birth, she went back to dancing. I knew that dancing made her heart sing, so, of course, I did not protest. For ten years, we lived a beautiful life as a family. But, the KGB was becoming more and more difficult to deal with, and my writing was bringing too much attention to us. Attention that I did not want for my two girls, but, nonetheless, it was there. Galina and I knew our time was very limited. It was only a matter of time before the KGB came for me. My writing and my ideas were the antithesis of what Communist Russia stood for. Talking about freedom of speech, human rights, and land ownership infuriated the politburo. The time had come to leave Russia, for our safety. I could not bear the thought of returning to the gulags or of having my wife and child imprisoned."

"How were you going to get out? I thought that, during those days, they killed people who tried to leave without permission," Katy said.

"*Da*, Katy, you are correct. We planned for months," Dimitri said. The lines on his face deepened as he spoke, and Katy could feel how heavily his decision still weighed on him.

"We had made all of the arrangements, and documents were created that would allow the three of us to be safely escorted across the eastern border. But, the day before we were supposed to obtain our documents, one of our accomplices, a dear friend, was arrested. Like that," he snapped his fingers, "our plans went up in smoke! We knew it was only a matter of hours before this man would be tortured into betraying us. To this day, I cannot think about what they did to him. It makes me ill to think about it. I never did find out," Dimitri said solemnly.

"What did you do?" Katy asked.

"The only thing we could do. We both knew that all three of us would never make it out without documents. If Galina stayed behind, she would have her career and a good life. The politburo had not identified her as a dissident. At least, that's what we thought. We argued over whether our darling Lena should stay or go. But, Lena was going to be a teenager soon, and the KGB did not hesitate to take young girls into the labor camps. And, they would have taken Lena to punish me. We agreed that Lena would come with me." Dimitri stopped and gazed at the flowers. He continued, "So we pretended it was just another night at the ballet. Lena was dancing the part of Clara in *The Nutcracker* with her mother." He smiled at the memory. "She was so happy to be dancing with her mother. Lena loved Galina so much and wanted to be just like her. It was an exciting night. I watched them both dance, and I almost forgot the horror that surrounded us in the beauty of that night. Lena and Galina were wonderful together. It was a spectacular evening," Dimitri said exuberantly.

"After the performance, I went backstage as usual to gather my girls and take them home. Only this time—if you could have seen the terror in Galina's beautiful green eyes—we spoke briefly, she had come up with a crazy plan. To this day I'm not sure how she thought of it. At the time, Russia was producing coal for most of Europe on the back of slave labor, and the coal trains ran in and out of the country on a daily basis. Galina had an engineer friend, Johann, who frequented the ballet whenever he was in town. She had seen him in the audience that night. So, she took my hand, and we went into the crowd and found him. Galina shared our story with him. I thought she was crazy, telling this stranger what we were planning. He could have yelled for the police right then and there, and it would have been over. But, he didn't. He took out a piece of paper and directed me to meet him at the address he had written down at midnight. Galina thanked him over and over again. He just smiled and said, 'Anything for the Great Galina.'" Dimitri stopped talking, shaking his head as if he thought that what he was saying was too incredulous to believe.

"We went backstage and found little Lena laughing and playing with some of the cast members. Oh, they loved her as much as they loved her mother. She looked so content and happy. I almost could not make myself do what I had to do next." Tears started running down his face.

"Galina called to her driver and asked him to take me and Lena to the address that Johann had given me. We both knew it was too risky to go home. We couldn't take that chance. The possibility that KGB thugs were waiting for us was too great. So, we bundled Lena up in Galina's big fur coat and wrapped her head with two woolen scarves. Lena was so happy her mother put her fur coat on her. She thought it made her look just like Galina. She had not worn galoshes that night, and I remember I was worried about her feet. But, Galina went to her dressing room and stuffed two pairs of warm slippers inside my coat pocket. I had only my wool coat, galoshes, and the clothes that I was wearing that evening. Galina walked us out to the car, and, there, I kissed my beloved wife goodbye. The plan was for Galina to use her prominence to set up a secondary plan to get out of Russia. She thought perhaps she could travel to a non-Soviet venue with the ballet and seek asylum. We promised that we would see each other soon, but it wasn't meant to be." Dimitri hung his head.

Katy thought, *He's been walking around with a broken heart all these years.* "Dimitri, you don't have to tell me if you don't want to," she said as she reached out and took his hand. "I can see how painful these memories are."

"Ah, Katy, someone should know my story before I go."

"Dimitri, don't talk like that," she said softly.

He just smiled at her and picked up where he had left off. "The driver dropped us off at the given address, a train station," Dimitri said. "I think he was suspicious because this was no place for a man with a ten-year-old girl, especially at that time of night. But, he left us and, in about an hour, Galina's engineer friend showed up. During this time, I was trying to keep a very exhausted Lena still while we waited. Fortunately, she fell asleep for a short time in my arms." Dimitri demonstrated how he had cradled Lena on his lap with his arms around her.

"The engineer told me the only safe place for us was going to be in the coal itself. Some of the cars were packed looser than others, and we were going to climb into this one particular car and hide. He told me the train was headed to Poland, and, from Poland, we would be able to find another train that would cross the eastern border. But, it would be very dangerous, as there were guards and dogs everywhere. He told me he thought I had a better chance of surviving dealing with the secret police than escaping but shrugged and showed me the car that we were supposed to climb into.

"I placed Lena on my back. By now, she was awake, and I told her, 'Hold on tight.' We climbed the car ladder probably thirty feet straight up. When I looked down and saw the coal, I was worried that we would be buried alive. But I did as he instructed. At first the coal seemed too hard-packed. I couldn't find a soft spot to dig into. And then, Lena started crying because she was hungry and wanted to go home. It never occurred to me that she probably didn't eat before her performance. Most dancers don't eat before they dance, you know," he said with great authority. "I almost turned back then, thinking about how my little girl was so hungry. But, I told her that if she sat quietly with me, I would find her something to eat in a little while."

Katy looked at him with a mix of horror and sadness.

"Finally, I dug out a place for both of us to sit somewhat protected from the wind but not protected from the cold. Russian winters are known for their unforgiving temperatures, and, as fate would have it, that night was a particularly brutal one. It brought back memories of the train ride to Kolyma. I pulled Lena close to me and told her to hang onto her Papa. Around three in the morning, the train suddenly jerked forward, and we started our journey to freedom."

Katy could tell he was exhausted and emotionally spent, but he continued with a clarity that she rarely saw in him anymore.

"After a long, arduous, and very cold train ride, through the grace of God and the kindness of strangers, we arrived in West Germany. Just outside the Berlin Wall was a refugee camp where we spent several months before we finally obtained our visas to come to America. I talked to everyone about Galina. Trying to find out what happened to her, trying to figure out how to get her to Germany so that we could travel to the United States together. Elena cried almost every day in the camps. She missed her mother and could not understand why she wasn't with us. She eventually concocted a story in her head and blamed me for 'forgetting' Galina and leaving her in Russia. I tried to explain to her that this was not true, but she was only ten. And, she needed a reason why her mother was not with her. So, I stopped denying it.

"We arrived in the United States, and I was immediately asked to become an interpreter for the American Consulate. We were still involved in the Cold War at that time, you know. Elena accused me of telling the Americans 'secrets' and betraying her mother. She would scream at me, 'Now, Momma will never be able to get to us!' and would storm off to her room. Perhaps she was right. Maybe the KGB did know I was working for the Americans, and maybe they did detain her. I was heartbroken, Katy. I lost my beloved Galina, and I lost my daughter all in the name of freedom. Your American soldiers are right. Freedom is not free. That first year here in the States was one of the worst. Thank God I found the studio for Elena. At least there she found something familiar, and they were Russian, like her. They taught her English and how to dance. The studio saved Lena during that awful time. I always felt like I had failed her, but I was so grateful she had them to turn to. But our relationship has always been . . . difficult."

Katy looked at him and said, "Well, despite the initial hardships in her life, Lena has done very well. Her studio is a success, she has many students who adore her, and I think she loves her work."

"*Da,* she does love her work, but I worry about her. Ever since we moved to the States, I have watched her cut herself off from her feelings. Sometimes, she does not see what is right in front of her, or she makes her life difficult because she refuses to acknowledge what her heart is telling her. Always trying to outrun the future and never letting go of the past, that's my Lena. It is no way to live, Katy. Her worst enemy is fear, and I am afraid she learned that from her parents."

Katy thought about what he said and then asked, "Did you ever find Galina?"

"No, my Galina was lost. Rumors made it back to me, but none of them were verifiable. I only hope and pray that she did not suffer the same fate as I did and get sent to a labor camp. For years, I was tortured by those thoughts. There is something to be said for losing some memories."

"Dimitri, I am so sorry. I can't even begin to imagine how difficult your life has been."

"Ekaterina, life is life. We have two choices, to live it or to leave it."

Katy sat with him, arm-in-arm, for another hour out in the garden under the cherry blossom tree in silence, listening to the stream, embracing the melancholy of the story she had just heard. She wondered what had really happened to Galina and if she was still alive. Her heart ached for Dimitri. *It couldn't have been easy with a young defiant teenager blaming him for her mother's absence*, she thought. *He has to be one of the bravest men*

I know. Which made her think of the question she was dreading asking him.

"Dimitri, what was Lena's married name?" she asked, holding her breath as she waited for the answer.

Dimitri turned to Katy and said, "Foster. Her husband's name was Jack Foster."

CHAPTER XVII

Behind the mask of ice that people wear,
there beats a heart of fire.

—PAULO COELHO

HARBOR PLACE
JULY 2013

Two weeks had passed since Dimitri confirmed Katy's suspicions. Jack was Elena's husband. She had made up multiple excuses not to go to the studio and work with Elena, but she knew that, eventually, she was going to have to decide what to do with the information. Katy felt guilty and would lie awake at night trying to decide whether to tell Elena or not. Losing Elena's friendship would be devastating. Before Elena, Katy had been loath to allow herself a friend after losing Shveta. But now she and Elena laughed together, shared stories of Dimitri's bad behavior, their favorite childhood memories, and conversations about the world in general. Katy had formed a bond of friendship with Elena, and she did not want to destroy it.

But, on the other hand, Katy knew she could not continue being Elena's friend without telling her. She felt deceitful for hiding such a secret from her. She either had to stop seeing Elena or tell her and face the consequences.

Katy spoke to Dr. Junger about her dilemma. "I don't know what to do with the knowledge of Jack's infidelity and how he died, Dr. Junger."

"Katy, do you think your moral dilemma is the root of your increased agitation?"

"What? No! . . . At least, I don't think so . . . I haven't really thought about it. I just attributed it to another go-round with flashbacks." Katy was surprised by the question.

"Katy, what is your agitation telling you? Are you agitated because you feel you are betraying a friend, or is Jack's betrayal causing this mental anguish?"

Katy thought for a moment and then said, "Ever since I got Jack's letter and found out he was Lena's husband . . . I've had a sick, nagging feeling in my stomach. I can't shake it," she said as she placed her hand on her belly. "My dreams used to be about war, bombs, and blood . . . Now they're about loss, deception, and grief."

"If you tell Elena the truth, how do you think your dreams will change, if at all?"

Katy hesitated for a moment and then spontaneously said, "I don't know how my dreams will change, but I will feel relieved."

"Why relieved?"

"Because I am being deceitful, just like Jack, and that is not who I am. My tolerance for the possible consequences of my revelation is higher than my tolerance for being a manipulative liar."

"Then there's your answer, Katy."

Katy left Junger's office dreading what she had to do.

She called Elena the next day and asked her to come to Harbor Place to talk. Elena agreed and came by that evening. It was still light outside, so Katy took Elena to the garden to talk in private. *Sunsets in this garden are so beautiful,* Katy thought as she guided Elena to her favorite spot under the cherry tree. "This is my favorite place in the whole garden. Your dad and I sit here a lot and talk."

"It's beautiful. . . But, Katy, what's going on? What did Papa do now?" Elena asked with a slight tone of annoyance in her voice.

"Oh, Lena, no, no, this isn't about your father. I actually haven't seen him today, but yesterday he was doing pretty well.

No, I have something very difficult to tell you, and I don't know how to start."

Katy could see Elena tense up. Her eyes grew serious and her lips tightened. "What's going on, Katy?"

"Lena, you know I was injured in Afghanistan, right?"

"Yes, of course . . . "

"I never told you that the injury happened in Kandahar, did I?"

"No . . . Kandahar, that's where Jack was killed."

"Lena, when I was stationed in Kandahar, I was seeing someone. I was in love with him . . . At the time I didn't know much about him, but we gave each other a lot of comfort and joy in a horrible place during a difficult time."

"I can't imagine how awful it must have been over there, Katy."

"Lena, I can't even begin to tell you . . . " Katy's voice faded off. "But that's not what I want to talk about."

Elena reached over and took Katy's hand. "Katy, just say what you need to say. I'm here for you."

Katy felt tears welling up in her eyes. She looked at her friend, and her heart broke in half as she said, "Lena, I was having an affair with your husband. I didn't know it at the time, Lena, I swear. He never told me."

Elena withdrew her hand. Katy could see her face change from puzzlement to recognition of what she had just heard.

Elena scowled and looked away. When she turned back to Katy, there were tears in her eyes. "Katy, how long have you known?"

"I've had a nagging feeling ever since we went to the park. I finally got up the courage to ask Dimitri what your married name was. He told me a couple of weeks ago. That's why I haven't been to see you. I just felt like such a traitor. But, there's more . . . "

Elena's tone turned sharp. "What else could there be, Katy? You slept with my husband." She threw her hands up in the air. Katy could see this was falling apart quickly.

"Lena, I was with Jack the night he was killed."

"What?"

"The night Jack was killed, we were out together with the team on a mission. Things went horribly wrong. Jack saw me running toward a minefield and jumped out of the helicopter, I think to try and stop me from running into an IED. At that moment, another IED went off, and he was killed. He died instantly. I was able to hold him in my arms for a brief moment. But, we were under fire, and I was pulled out. I had to leave him lying there," Katy said, tears streaming down her face. She waited for the information to sink in.

Elena stood up from the bench. Looking squarely at Katy and with rage in her voice, Elena said, "I always knew there was someone else in Jack's life, but I could never prove it. Do you have any idea the heartache and anguish you have caused me? How your deceit wrecked my marriage? For the longest time I thought it was me, that I wasn't good enough for Jack, and that was why he rejected me. Now, I find out it was *you*! I want to hurt you, Katy, like you have never been hurt before, so you can experience the pain I felt. I can't believe you—I allowed you into my life, you were my friend . . . I never want to see you again!" Elena screamed at her. The last two years of the mental agony, grief, and sorrow her marriage had caused her poured out in her anger.

"Lena, please wait, I didn't know . . . I swear, I didn't know."

"*Shlyukha!*[16] You were there when my husband died, and you don't tell me until now? Then you tell me you were having an affair with him? Really? What else do you know that I should know? Was he planning on leaving me for you?" she said as she slammed her fist down on the bench's armrest. "You are dead to me, and stay away from my father," she screamed as she ran out of the garden.

"Lena, please wait," Katy pleaded. But Elena did not stop. As Katy sobbed, uncontrollably, the air in the atrium shifted, and, suddenly, thousands of cherry blossom petals floated softly to the ground, covering it in a carpet of pink and white blossoms.

16　Whore!

It's Shveta all over again. I'm still spilling blood, Katy thought as the petals drifted down like snow.

Sitting there, consumed by her emotions, she hoped for some comfort. *Where is Dimitri? He always knows when I'm out here and upset. Did Elena tell him not to talk to me anymore?* That thought started another round of sobs. Finally, exhausted, she dragged herself back to her room feeling abandoned and brokenhearted.

CHAPTER XVIII

A great man does not seek applause or place;
he seeks for truth; he seeks the road to happiness,
and what he ascertains, he gives to others.

—ROBERT GREEN INGERSOLL

HARBOR PLACE LOBBY
JULY 2013

Amanda Jones was seventeen years old, just old enough to hold a job, but young enough, still, to be oblivious and irresponsible. Her mother, a nurse at Harbor Place, had twisted HR's arm into giving her daughter the front-desk receptionist job that was available. Amanda really didn't want to be spending after-school hours working, but her mother thought this was the only way to keep her wayward daughter out of trouble. So, Amanda was the first face that people saw when they entered Harbor Place.

Her job was not complicated. She said hello and smiled when people entered the building, inquired about their reason for being there, and issued them a visitor sticker with their name on it. Notifying administrative staff, when salespeople or other business personnel showed up, was also part of her job. Unfortunately, Amanda was more interested in the boys she met at school than her job. Worse yet, she couldn't spell.

Her supervisor, Quincy Jackson, was appalled when she was introduced to him as the new receptionist. HR had taken him aside and told him to "let her hang herself," so that her mother couldn't whine to HR further when she was let go. But, in the meantime, Quincy had to put up with her endless errors and difficult behavior. If he heard her say "like" one more time, he thought he might have to commit homicide. Her bad habit of trying to cover up her mistakes with self-effacing comments like "Oh, it's like I never went to school," when she misspelled someone's name, drove him crazy. Whenever she was asked to do something she didn't want to do, she would sarcastically say, "Like I would know how to do that." Quincy was on edge and counting the days before she screwed up enough so that he could finally let her go.

At the time of Katy's conversation with Elena, Quincy came out of his office to see a line six people deep at the front desk and Amanda scribbling furiously on an ID sticker. He noticed she had three or four crumbled up next to her. The group in front of the desk appeared to be quite agitated. Quincy once again went over to dig Amanda out. Shaking his head in dismay, he straightened out the mess and got everyone processed. Under his glare, Amanda started to cry. Quincy just rolled his eyes and walked back to his office.

Unfortunately, what neither of them noticed during all the chaos was an elderly male resident slip out the front door. Unbeknownst to the staff, Dimitri had slipped into a delusional state and wandered out the door.

Once free, he walked for several hours, asking passersbys if they had seen Galina. "Pardon me, madam, have you seen the great Galina?" he asked in Russian. "Excuse me, sir, I'm looking for Galina. Have you seen her?" he asked over and over again. It was growing dark and cold. He wandered into an alley and saw some movement behind a trash container. Bending over, he found a feral cat that was looking for a meal. As he picked it up, the cat bit him and scratched his hand and face, so he dropped it and watched it run off. Confused, Dimitri continued to walk.

Back at Harbor Place it was dinnertime, and Katy came out of her room looking for Dimitri. After her conversation with Elena, she really wanted to talk to him. But, he didn't show up for dinner. "Anna, have you seen Dimitri?" she asked one of the nurses.

"No, honey, he's probably in his room asleep. He's been sleeping a lot lately."

That sounded plausible to Katy, so she went over to her table to eat. Dimitri had been sleeping a lot lately, and Katy was worried about him. After eating, she decided to check on him to make sure he was OK. Knocking on his door, she received no answer. Normally, she would have left him alone, but something told her to knock again. Still no answer, so she opened the door very slowly. She didn't want to scare him if he was in there. "Dimitri are you here?" she asked almost in a whisper.

She received no answer. She felt a small prick of fear and reached for the light switch near the door. The room was empty. Katy quickly went out to the garden to look for him there, worried he might be lying on the ground unable to get up. But, he was not there either. Alarmed, she went back to Anna.

"Anna, Dimitri is missing." she said, visibly shaken.

"What are you talking about, Katy?"

"Anna, I can't find him anywhere. He's not in his room, and he's not out in the garden. I'm worried. Do you think he's escaped again?"

"Oh Lord!" Anna said. "Jackie, have you seen Dimitri today?" she asked one of the aides.

"No ma'am, I haven't."

"Katy, when was the last time you saw him?"

"I saw him this morning right after breakfast. I was a little worried about him because he didn't look well and was a little confused. I thought he was resting this afternoon and that's why he wasn't around."

"All right, honey, thank you. Don't worry, we'll find him. We always do," she said. "He really hasn't been himself the last couple of days. Let me go notify the supervisor."

Feeling helpless, Katy watched Anna walk toward the supervisor's office. Dimitri had been quite tearful the last couple of days. Katy thought maybe he was coming down with something, or perhaps telling his story about Galina had taken an emotional toll. She yelled after Anna, "Someone should call Elena."

Anna turned to acknowledge her and, then, disappeared down the hall.

The police found Dimitri slumped over on a park bench twenty-four hours later, around three in the morning. There was no telling how long he had been there, but it was obvious he was seriously ill. An ambulance was called, and he was taken to the emergency room. The authorities called the nursing home, and they, in turn, called Elena.

Andrei had been at Elena's side while the authorities searched for Dimitri. When Elena got the call saying they had found him, Andrei called Miss Laura from the daycare and asked if she could pick up the twins. They drove to the hospital as soon as the kids were picked up, a feeling of dread hanging in the air.

At the hospital emergency room, they were immediately escorted to the stretcher where Dimitri was lying. *He looks so pale*, Lena thought. She turned to Andrei. "He has always been larger than life to me, Andrei. Now look at him," she whispered. "Papa, can you hear me? It's Lena," she said as she reached down and took his hand. It was ice cold. A momentary flashback—his hand had been cold like this when they rode in the coal train together. She had cried because she couldn't get him to wake up. Elena gasped and withdrew her hand from his, instantly.

"What is it, Lena?" Andrei asked.

Shaking her head, she said, "Nothing, just . . . an old memory," and picked up his hand again. "*Papulia*, open your eyes. Please, Papa, I want to see those eyes," she pleaded. As tears streamed down her face, she said, "Papa, I love you . . . please don't leave me. You are all I have left. Sasha and Tasha need you—I need you."

"Galina?" Dimitri whispered. "*Gde* Galina?"[17]

"No, Papa, it's me, Lena." She brought his hand to her face.

"Ahh, Galina, there you are. I have been looking everywhere for you. Where have you been?" His eyes were opened but were glazed over.

"Papa, Momma is not here, it's your *ziechick*."

"*Moy ziechick*?"

"Yes, Papa, your little bunny. I am here."

---

17   Where is Momma?

"*Ziechick, gde Mamulia?*" Dimitri asked.

"Papa, Momma is . . . " Elena thought quickly. "Momma went to get potatoes for the soup."

"Ahh, soup tonight, that's good. Did you dance today, my little Lena? What did your mother say?"

"Yes, Papa, I danced today, and Momma was happy."

Tears welled up in Dimitri's eyes and ran down the sides of his face. "I should have never left her there. I should not have left her there."

"Papa?"

"They took her, my Galina, they took her and like a dog sent her to the gulag. Oh, Galina, why didn't you come with me?"

"Gulag, Papa? What are you talking about?"

Tears were streaming, but Dimitri had used up the last of his energy. The cat bite had infected his bloodstream almost immediately, and now he was septic. His blood pressure was low, his temperature high, and he was cold and clammy. His heart was weak and fighting a losing battle to keep blood flowing despite the antibiotics and fluids. There was nothing more that could be done. The doctor said only time would tell, but Elena already knew the outcome of this journey.

There they sat, Dimitri and Elena hand in hand, with Elena's other hand in Andrei's. Three hearts connected by grace, a force that does not speak but embraces all that it surrounds, its only function to comfort as lives are changed.

—

News of Dimitri's death quickly spread to the nursing home. Anna made a special trip to Katy's room to tell her and held her as Katy cried for the loss of her friend. Katy asked Anna if she could go to Dimitri's room and sit in there for a little while. Anna said, "Yes, of course."

In Dimitri's room was a picture that was special to Katy. As she entered his room, she felt a strange sense of serenity. She thought to herself, *Dimitri, are you with Galina now? I hope so. I know how much you loved her.* This thought actually made her feel a tiny bit better. Looking around the room, she was struck by how minimally he lived. There was a picture of Elena on his bedside table. Katy saw a pair of black boots that he liked and a couple of pairs of pants hanging in the closet. There were several framed pictures of Russian artwork and multiple books in Russian, but other than that he did not have anything of any real value. Then she saw the picture on top of his dresser, a small framed picture of a painting of an elegant, beautiful woman. She was wearing a ball gown and had beautiful long blonde hair covered by a diamond-studded tiara. Posing with a gorgeous smile, she was the picture of elegance. The caption on the picture read, *Ekaterina, Grand Czarina, Mother Russia,*

1762–1796. Holding the small picture next to her heart, Katy sat with Dimitri in spirit one last time and wept.

—

His memorial was held in a Russian Orthodox Church with vaulted ceilings and beautiful stained-glass windows surrounding the altar. The choir sang songs in Russian, and the service was solemn and beautiful. During his lifetime, Dimitri had made many friends. Many of his peers were gone, but their children still remembered him. The son of one of the diplomats Dimitri had worked closely with when he first came to America sat in a pew with his children. Many of the parents from Elena's studio were incredibly generous with flower contributions, and the room was filled with the scent of lilies, white gardenias, and roses. Anna, from Harbor Place, attended the memorial and brought Katy with her. Katy wasn't sure how it would go over with Elena, given their last encounter, but she wanted to pay her respects to Dimitri. She also had something for Elena.

Katy cried as the choir sang their songs. She had no idea what they were saying, but the music was mournful and emotional. There were many accolades for his work as a dissident and his bravery for escaping Soviet Russia. People from the studio talked about how he had been so good to their children. Finally, Andrei got up and spoke about how he had first met Elena at the studio, and he blessed her father for bringing her there that fateful day. All in all, the service was a lovely memorial for the larger-than-life Dimitri.

Katy had purposefully placed herself at the end of the receiving line. She waited an hour and half as people paid their respects to Elena, with Andrei standing at her side. Katy thought her turn to greet Elena would be awkward, but Elena was subdued in her grief.

Walking up to greet them both, Katy said, "Lena, I'm so sorry for your loss."

Elena leaned in as if she was going to growl something ugly but instead took Katy's hand and said, "Katy, thank you for coming. My father loved you. You were a bright light for him, and I think you gave him great comfort while he was at Harbor Place."

Katy stared at her in disbelief but quickly composed herself. "Lena, I don't know what this is, but Dimitri asked that I give this to you if anything were to happen to him." She handed Elena an envelope.

Elena eyed it suspiciously for a moment but took it from Katy. "Thank you," she whispered through tears.

"Lena . . . one other thing. If you are ever interested, he told me the story of your escape from Russia and about your mother. Someday, if you would like to hear his version, I would be happy to share it with you. You should know his bravery and courage helped kick me out of my funk and allowed me to move forward.

I just thought you would like to know that your Dad changed one more life before he passed."

"*Spaciba*,[18] Katy. I . . . " Elena could not continue. Andrei put his arm around her, and she leaned into his shoulder to cry.

Gently touching Elena's arm, Katy said, "May you find peace, Lena." And with that, she left.

---

18 Thank you

CHAPTER XIX

In spite of everything I still believe that people are really good at heart. I simply can't build up my hopes on a foundation consisting of confusion, misery, and death.

—ANNE FRANK

DANCE STUDIO
END OF JULY 2013

Two weeks later, the bustle from the funeral had died down, and Elena was trying hard to get back to normal life. As usual, Andrei was accommodating and had taken over most of her lessons in addition to teaching his own. He helped her with the twins and spent most of his free time at Elena's house.

That day, she walked into her office, and she noticed the manila envelope where she had left it on top of the filing cabinet. *Papa's notes?* Elena wondered. *Do I want to open this now? Do I have the strength?* With a big sigh, she plopped down into her office chair, envelope in hand, just as Andrei walked by the office door.

"Andrei, do you have a few minutes before your lessons?" she asked.

He stopped and smiled at her and said, "No, Lena, they're here already. What's up?"

"Oh, I just thought you would sit with me while I open this envelope from Papa."

"Tell you what, let's do it together tonight at the house. We'll get the twins tucked in and then we can spend time with whatever it was that Dema wanted you to have."

She inhaled deeply and said, "You're right, this is better opened at home. Let's just get through the day."

They both had lessons booked for the entire day, and it passed by quickly. During Elena's last lesson, Andrei picked up the twins, and, by the time he returned to the studio, she was ready to go.

"Do you have your envelope, Lena?" he asked gently.

"Right here in my purse. How was your day, my little munchkins?" She smiled at the twins sitting in the back seat.

"We were *great*, Momma, except Sasha ate a bug!"

"Yeah, but Tasha tried to eat clay, and the teacher wouldn't let her."

Both kids then started giggling, and the car was filled with a joy that Elena had not felt in a long time. By the time they got home, everyone was in a great mood and ready for supper.

"So, do you want to cook or play?" Andrei asked as they walked in the front door.

"I think I would like to cook. Do you mind?" she asked as she looked at the twins.

"No problem. OK guys, Mom is going to cook us something special tonight, and we are going to go play upstairs while she cooks."

"Yay!" the twins cheered and went scrambling up the stairs.

"If you don't hear from me soon, send out the rescue squad, Lena," he said, laughing as he went up the stairs.

Elena walked into the kitchen and found herself humming a popular song she had just heard on the radio. She pulled out the ingredients for borscht and started cutting up the vegetables for the soup. She thought, *This was always Papa's favorite meal. I wonder if Momma used to make it for him.* She smiled at the thought and pulled the meal together with great ease.

"OK, guys, wash your hands and let's eat," she yelled up the stairs as she set the last bowl on the table.

She heard thunderous footsteps come running down the staircase. *If only I had that much energy,* she thought as she rolled her eyes and smiled.

After everyone was seated and served, Elena looked at Andrei, picked up her glass, and said, "Here's to this family. May we always remember how important we are to each other, and may we never forget Grandpa."

Andrei looked at her and smiled. "To Dema!"

"To Dema!" said the twins with much laughter as they used their grandfather's first name.

"To Dimitri Victorvich Demidova," said Elena. "OK, guys, eat up and we can have dessert."

The meal was simple, but it was one of those family meals that would live on in their collective memories for many years to come. After Elena and Andrei got the twins to bed, he poured her a glass of wine and brought the envelope to her as they sat on the couch.

"Andrei, I don't know if I want to open this. I don't want to spoil such a wonderful night."

"Don't worry, Lena, I have a feeling Dema left you something special, and I will be right here for you." He reached over and squeezed her hand.

"As always, Andrei. As always."

The envelope was very light. She gently broke the seal so as not to ruin it. She looked inside and pulled out another envelope and some pictures. As she turned the pictures over, she gasped. "Oh my God, Andrei, look!"

There were several pictures, big and small, but there was one eight-by-ten that had captured her attention. It was a black-and-white picture of her and her mother taking their final bow after their *Nutcracker* performance all those years ago. Lena looked at her mother in the picture and felt like she was looking in a mirror. She also noticed what a young girl she had been at that time. In her mind, she had always felt older when they ran away from Russia. The stage they were standing on was ornate, and the curtains were heavy velour with satin sashes. The cast stood behind her and her mother with big smiles, and, in one corner, she could see the director peeking out from backstage, looking quite proud.

"Lena, is that you?" Andrei asked.

"Andrei, this is the last time I ever saw my mother. We performed *The Nutcracker,* and I danced the part of Clara. Look how beautiful she is. How did Papa ever get this picture?" She turned it over. There was a notation written in Russian on the back. *Per your request, Dimitri.*

"I don't know, but you look just like your mother, Lena," he said and brushed his hand gently across her cheek.

"Oh, Andrei, look, this is Papa and Momma together. See how happy they look," she said, surprised as she picked up another picture.

"Why do you say it like that, Lena?"

"Because if they were so happy, why would he leave her behind? It doesn't make any sense."

"Lena, I still think there is more to the story than you remember. Do you remember Katy saying Dema told her the story of your escape, and, if you wanted to hear it, she would be happy to share it with you?"

"Yes, I do," she said cautiously.

"Are you ready to hear it?"

She looked at him, wide-eyed. "I'm . . . umm . . . do you think she can tell me something I don't know?"

"You will never know, Lena, unless you talk to her."

She looked at him and, then, back at the pictures. Pictures of her mother and father, of the three of them as a family. There they were, laughing, eating, and being together. When were these taken? Why didn't she remember these moments? Had her anger been so intense she had eliminated the good memories? These were beautiful pictures, and they had the same feel to them as tonight's family dinner—family, life, love, and belonging. How could she have forgotten these moments from so long ago in her own childhood?

For most of the evening, she sat with Andrei and talked about the pictures. She remembered things in the pictures that surprised her, including family members she had not thought about or heard from since she was a child. She and Andrei laughed at the crazy memories the pictures ignited. They talked for hours about their Russian families and found they shared many of the same family rituals and traditions.

By the end of the night, Elena knew two things. She loved Andrei with all her heart, and she would eventually have to talk to Katy.

CHAPTER XX

Integrity =
(Intention + Discipline) (Love + Forgiveness + Compassion)

—C.M. SCHAFFER

TIME TO SAY GOODBYE
AUGUST 2013

Katy's time at Harbor Place had come to an end. The benefits of her physical therapy had been accelerated by the dance technique Lena had taught her, and she no longer used her wheelchair. Her flashbacks had diminished, and she had become quite adept at handling them when they occurred. She and Dr. Junger agreed they had more than accomplished the goals they had set, and he discharged her from his care. She finalized her plans to return to California. Her father was encouraging her to pick up where she had left off with her writing, but Katy was thinking about doing something completely different.

Dimitri had been dead for almost a month, and Harbor Place did not feel the same without him. Katy missed him, their daily talks in the garden, his stories of Russia and his family, and even his confused memories. She missed hearing him call her Ekaterina.

She had not realized how important the nickname he had given her on that first night was to her. The picture of the Czarina Ekaterina was on her bedside table. It was her daily reminder of Dimitri, his strength and courage and, above all, his faith in her.

Telling Elena about Jack had been one of the hardest things Katy had ever done in her life. But, in the end, she was glad she had told her the truth. Dimitri once told her, "The great Mark Twain said, 'When in doubt, tell the truth.'" She smiled at the thought of that crazy Russian man knowing who Mark Twain was. *He was well read, wasn't he*, she thought.

In her last session with Dr. Junger, Katy reflected back on the crooked path of her journey so far. "You know, Doc, it's been a pretty amazing experience. Over the last four months, I watched Dimitri try to escape the pain from a horrible decision he was forced to make so many years ago. I saw Lena fighting her anger at her father and then unleashing it on me, and I guess I've just been trying to escape a finite truth. Each of us was looking for relief from pain, trying to find a way back to solid ground. What do you think, Doc? Were we the Lion, the Scarecrow, and the

Letters of Forgiveness

Tin Man? I mean, really, what are the chances the three of us would be thrown together? It's crazy, isn't it, how the universe puts people in our lives?"

Dr. Junger smiled and wished her well. "I think you will probably have more journeys like this one if you are open to it, Katy. You know I am only a phone call away if you need me. But for now, I wish you well."

Katy was grateful for the closure she was getting at Harbor Place. But there was one more thing she needed to do. *I can't leave here without telling Elena how sorry I still am*, she thought as she sat down at her desk to pen a letter to Elena.

Dearest Lena,

I'm not sure how to even begin this letter. I'm not even sure you will read it, but I have to at least try to tell you how sorry I am. Your friendship and your father's friendship changed my life, and I can't leave without acknowledging that to you. I can't imagine how I would have survived Harbor Place without the two of you.

I know I should have told you about Jack as soon as I found out, but I'm not sure it would have changed the outcome. You would still have felt betrayed, and rightfully so. Lena, the hardest thing I have ever done in my life was telling you that I had an affair with your husband and that I was there when he was killed. I'd have rather given up my other leg than have to tell you about it.

Before I met you and your family, I would have said I understood Jack and knew him well. But knowing what I know now about you and the twins makes me wonder what was really going on in his head. He had a beautiful wife and family. Why would he want to mess that up?

Lena, I don't have answers, just more questions to pile on to your questions, I'm sure. What I do know is neither of us deserved to be treated the way Jack treated us. I deserved the truth, and you deserved a committed husband. Neither one of us got what we should have.

We will never know what was truly going on in his head. All I know is that he took risks he didn't need to take, he lived a lie, and he left behind a lot of questions that will never be answered, at least not to our satisfaction.

But what I do want to say is, I'm sorry. I'm sorry for your losses, Jack, your father, your faith in me. Losses that can't be recovered, losses that will color your life forever, losses that bear a huge weight on both of our hearts.

I want you to know I cherished the time we spent together, laughing and joking, working, and pushing hard for results. I miss your camaraderie and your constant pushing to make me a whole person again. I know now you saw something in me that I couldn't see in myself at the time.

I can only hope that, as time goes on, your opinion of me will soften and your memories will be of the good times we shared together. I will always remember the first step I took on my own in your studio, with all your other students cheering me on. This memory will forever have a special place in my heart. It was the moment when I started to believe again. I hope when you think of me you will remember the day we all went to the park and watched Dimitri come alive with the twins. I think he became a little boy again that day. It was beautiful to see. So many fond memories for such a short period of time.

I know this may not be the right time for this, but I needed to let you know before I return to California. I never meant to hurt you, and the saddest part of my stay here in Washington has been the loss of you and your father. Please know you will always be someone I admire and respect. The time we had together was special, Lena, and I will never forget it.

> *I hope someday you find peace with all that has happened.*
>
> *Katy*

—

That afternoon Katy said her goodbyes to all the staff who'd been part of her life for the last four months. It was harder than she thought it would be. She went back to Dr. Junger's office and gave him a huge hug. "Thank you," was all she could get out. The staff at Harbor Place were kind people trying to make a difference in others' lives, and Katy respected them for that. Shame washed over her as she thought about her first four weeks there and how difficult she had been.

Thinking about all that had happened, she knew in her heart it had been Dimitri who truly helped her find herself again. She whispered a prayer, "Wherever you are, Dimitri, may you be at peace. You will always be in my heart. I owe you so much."

As she took her final steps out of Harbor Place, she placed Elena's letter in the outgoing mailbox, turned for one last look at the lobby, and then walked out to the waiting taxi. She was finally going home.

Epilogue

EPILOGUE

Forgiveness is giving up the hope that the past
could have been any different.
—Oprah Winfrey

ONE YEAR LATER
ELENA'S HOUSE

A brisk fall evening had the wind whipping leaves around in the yard. Sasha and Tasha had been outside with Andrei for more than an hour. After dinner they fell asleep on the living room floor, and Andrei carried them up to bed. Elena was in the kitchen opening a bottle of wine to share with him when he returned. They were about to celebrate their one-month anniversary as a married couple when the doorbell rang. "Andrei, can you get that?"

"I got it," he replied as he bounded down the stairs.

Elena heard the door open and then surprise in Andrei's voice. She heard a voice that sounded familiar, but she couldn't quite place it. Walking out to the living room, she stopped short when she saw Katy in the foyer. There was an elderly woman with her as well.

"Katy . . . ?" she said as she stiffened. "What are you doing here?"

"Hello, Lena. I heard you and Andrei got married. Congratulations."

"Thank you, but surely you didn't come all this way to say congratulations?"

"No. No, I did not. I came all this way because I wanted you to meet someone," Katy said, looking over at the older woman who now inexplicably had tears running down her face.

"Lena, this nice lady only speaks Russian, so it was a little difficult to convince her to come with me. But, I would like you to ask her what her name is. In Russian, please."

"Katy, what are you doing?" she demanded.

"Please, Lena, just bear with me. Ask her name."

Elena turned to the woman and said, "*Kak vas zovut?*"[19]

Through her tears, the woman replied, "My name is Galina Demidova. I am your mother."

---

19 "What is your name?"

Silence and shock filled the room. Stunned, Elena looked at Katy in disbelief as her hand came up to cover her mouth. Andrei looked just as shocked but intervened and asked the women to come in.

"Katy, please, both of you sit. I guess you have a story to share?" he asked as he first escorted the elderly woman and then Elena, who still had not spoken, to a chair. He sat on the armrest of Elena's chair.

"I'm sorry to just drop this on you, but I have been dying to tell you since the day I found her. When I returned to California, all I could do was think about Dimitri and how he never knew what happened to Galina."

Hearing her name, the old woman looked around to see if she could understand. Noticing her confusion, Andrei moved to sit with Galina and interpret as Katy spoke.

"I spent a month crying and wallowing in self-pity, kind of like how your father first found me. But then I thought, you know, maybe I can find out what happened to Galina for Dimitri's sake, and for you, Lena. So, I decided to use my skills as a journalist to get to the end of the story. I wrote letters to the state department, I used my military connections to research government documents, and I convinced people to give me information that they shouldn't have. But, I had to know what happened after you and your father left the theater that night so many years ago. I almost fell over dead when I found out Galina was here in the States. One day I was looking through some government documents, and there she was! In Virginia! For almost five years now. I couldn't believe it. Five years and Dimitri never knew. I did some more research to make sure it was her, and, sure enough, I had found your mother. Last week I flew out to Virginia to talk to her and share my stories of Dimitri with her. I also told her about you. I asked if she would like to come with me to meet you. She was so unsure because, if I understood the interpreter correctly, she has blamed herself all these years for not going with you when you left. She told me your father begged her to come. But, she refused. But, maybe I should let her tell you the story." In perfect Russian, Katy said, "Galina, tell Lena what happened that night."

"Katy, your Russian . . . " Andrei said.

"I've learned a few phrases," Katy said with a shrug and a smile.

Trembling, Galina began her story. "Lena, you need to know, your father did not purposely leave me behind. We were so in love, but unless you lived with the kind of fear your father and I faced daily, you could never understand the intense pressure that influenced our decisions. Living in fear is not living. We knew it was only a matter of time before he would be arrested again. His writing was so radical and so far from what the government allowed at the time. His greatest fear was not that he would be arrested but that they would arrest you and use you to hurt him. Your father had seen many young boys and girls in the gulags while he was there. He did not want that for you, and neither did I. We had planned to leave together, but one of the people helping us acquire documents was captured by the KGB. We knew the night of *The Nutcracker* we had to move. We just didn't know how because our original plan had been to leave with forged documents."

Andrei now interpreted for Katy as Galina spoke. Still, Elena sat listening in silence.

"That night, after the program, your father begged me to come with him. But I was too afraid. Looking back, I know it was the most difficult thing he ever had to do, but I insisted he go. I did not believe the three of us would be able to get out of the country together. I thought your father would have a much better chance, and I wanted you to go with him. Once he left, you would never be safe from the KGB if you remained with me. We cried together as we hugged and kissed each other with promises that we would be together again. With that, he went out the back door of the theater with you and left. What happened to the two of you afterward I didn't know. I was told you both had been captured and sent to the gulags, but, obviously, you were safe because here you are," she said with a sad smile.

Visibly shaken, with tears in her eyes, Elena said in Russian, "Momma, what happened to you? Papa looked for you for years. In fact, his last dying breath was for Galina. Why didn't you come to us? I missed you so much."

"My darling Lena, you cannot possibly remember the reign of terror in Russia at that time. Human rights, you take them for granted in this country, and you have grown up free. But, at that time in Russia, such things were never expected. Your father's writing was the only thing that kept the concept alive for us while he was there."

Andrei interrupted, "I'm so sorry, we have been rude. Can I get you some tea, Galina? Katy?"

Both women said yes, and he went to the kitchen to make tea. As he did, Elena picked up a picture of the twins and said to her mother, "You are a *babushka*[20], Momma."

A look of pure delight lit up Galina's face, and she asked their names.

"Alexander and Natalia."

"Ooh, Sasha and Tasha, *da*?"

"*Da*, Momma, Sasha, and Tasha."

Andrei came in with a tea set that looked very old and very Russian. It had been handed down to him from his family when he married Elena. The cups were traditional tea cups painted

---

20 Grandmother

with the palace of the last czars. It was a beautiful serving set. Andrei poured for everyone.

"Momma, what happened to you?" Elena asked.

"I was so worried about you two, but my engineer friend, Johann, was worried about me and insisted I was in danger, too. When he returned to the theater after seeing you and your father off at the train station, he insisted I needed to leave there and then. For a brief moment, I thought he was going to come up with a scheme to get me out, but that was not to be. He told me, 'Get into my car now!' and I obeyed him. I was too emotional to think clearly. We drove for two days straight only stopping briefly at very isolated spots along the way. I started to get scared because he would not tell me where we were going. In fact, I was thinking of a plan to escape when we arrived at our destination. He had brought me to a nunnery high up in the mountains above Moscow. I never knew people even lived that far up in the hills. But, there was this old castle inhabited by nuns. We walked up to the front gate. I thought it was odd no one came to greet us, but he rang the bell three times. Suddenly the gate opened, and he pushed me through. He told me I would be safe there, but he could go no further. It was for the nuns' protection and my own. I stayed there for almost eighteen years. I loved the nuns. They were kind and generous to me. We had very little, and, at times, we were starving. But, we had each other, and

I was safe. When Perestroika came, I was finally free to leave. There were many kisses goodbye, and, as soon as I exited that gate, they disappeared inside. I know they are still there."

"Momma, that's incredible. How did you get back to Moscow?"

"So much had changed since I had arrived at the nunnery. There were many roads coming and going, and a friendly man that I met at one of the rest stops took me into Moscow. I didn't recognize anything when I got there. I was so confused and frightened. I did not know how to get in touch with anyone that I used to know, and I had given up on ever seeing you or your father again."

Elena reached over and covered Galina's hand with hers. "Papa always told me that you were very strong and, eventually, you would find your way to us. I'm just sorry I never believed him. I'm sorry for many things right now."

Galina smiled at her daughter. "Life is for learning, my child. Your father always said that."

Elena smiled in recognition. "Yes, he did."

Andrei turned his attention to Katy and asked, "So, how did the two of you meet?"

Katy sighed and shrugged her shoulders. "Well, I just kept looking through document after document when one day I saw a visa application for Galina Demidova, age seventy-six. I thought, 'Oh my God! Is it possible? Could it be?' I can't tell you how fast my heart was racing when I found her address and located a phone number. Unfortunately, when I first called, we could not communicate. It took almost a week before someone was in the house who could interpret. It was the longest week of my life!"

Galina laughed as Andrei interpreted what Katy was saying.

"Finally, I made arrangements to go visit her. I did not want to involve you if she wasn't willing, and I had to be sure. But as soon as I saw those eyes, Lena, I knew she was your mother. You have your mother's eyes. Anyway, she offered me tea, and, as soon as I told her about you and Dimitri, she wanted to know how quickly we could go. I told her I had to make some flight arrangements, but we would go as soon as possible. By the way, she is living with a lovely Russian family as an au pair. They have two small children, and she stays in the house to care for them. I think she may be teaching them to dance, but I might have misunderstood that piece."

"*Da, da*," Galina said in response to Andrei's interpretation. "*Tanzevant, da.*"[21]

"She said, 'Yes, yes, dance.' You are correct, Katy," Andrei said.

"Anyway, so here we are," Katy said.

"Katy, why . . . ?" Elena asked, still looking quite bewildered.

---

21 "Dance, yes."

"Because, Lena, despite what you thought of me, I loved your father dearly, and the thought of you and I never seeing each other again was just too sad. Your family is part of me now, and I couldn't just let it end like it did. For Dimitri, I needed to solve the mystery of what happened to Galina, and I needed to resolve his daughter's questions. I told you that I hoped you would find peace, and I meant it. But, what if I could bring you that peace? Isn't that what a good friend would do?"

Elena just shook her head, tears streaming down her face. "I don't know what to say, Katy. I'm so sorry for the way I have treated you. After I read the letter you sent me, I knew I was wrong to be angry with you. I was ashamed of how I behaved that day."

"I know, Lena. We were both fooled by someone we cared for. But this," Katy gestured around, looking at Andrei and Galina and their home, "this is the real thing. Treasure this, Lena. People die for what you have here. This is your chance to live the life your father wanted for you."

Elena looked at her mother and said, "*Mamulia*, I have missed you so very much, and I always blamed Papa for not bringing you here with us."

"Elena," Galina said, using her daughter's formal name, "your father and I made a decision as your parents. The best one we could make with what we had and knew at the time. We did what we thought was best. I brought something with me that has been hidden for many years. Before we left for *The Nutcracker* that night, your Papa had composed one last letter. We placed it in a box, and I took it out into the backyard where there was an old smokehouse for curing meat. Papa had loosened several of the bricks where he stored copies of his papers. When I returned to Moscow, one of the things I wanted to do was to see if I could find it. The place where we had lived had turned into a slum, but the smokehouse was still there. I couldn't believe it! I went over to the place where the bricks were loose, and, to my surprise, they came right out and there was the box, just lying there where we had left it. The papers were old, mildewed, and yellowed from time and moisture. But, they were intact. I collected them and took them with me. I brought them with me to the United States because I knew they would be safe here. Please, Lena, let me read the last one he ever wrote while in Russia."

Elena nodded her head in agreement. Galina started to read, and Andrei sat next to Katy quietly interpreting.

Many years ago, I was imprisoned unjustly, without  *the right to a trial or the right to face my accusers or to see my family ever again. My life was forever changed in just a few short hours. During that time as a young man, I watched them mercilessly beat my father for no reason except to see him bleed. He eventually died because of those beatings, but, during all of the torment, starvation, and pain he endured, he never, never once stopped encouraging me to remember what was good in life. He died broken in body but not in spirit.*

During my imprisonment, they tried to make me cower but couldn't because my captors were unable to take away my ability to think, pray, and reflect. Because of this, I was able to celebrate a basic freedom every day during my imprisonment. No mortal hands could remove my intention to live with dignity and thoughtfulness.

When you are a prisoner, you learn to appreciate those things that are most worthwhile. Of course, the most worthwhile things in life are often the most difficult to achieve. Forgiveness, unconditional love, family, happiness—these are the things worth personal sacrifice. They cannot be found in another's backyard or in someone's pocketbook.

Spending ten years in a gulag taught me life does not wait. I was fortunate—ten years later, I was able to leave the wretched place that tried to steal my soul, and, in my beautiful Galina, I found those things that made life worthwhile again. Without her, I don't think I would have recovered my will to live after my release. Her, and my daughter, for whom I would willingly die—these are the people who have made my life worthwhile once again.

When we talk of breaking the chains of human misery, we are talking about reaching out to the worn and tired masses and recognizing that fame and fortune are not the ideals that sustain a country. It is the basic human essentials that maintain and sustain life. Our government is not responsible for ensuring our celebrity or our riches. It is only responsible for ensuring our ability to fulfill our obligations to those we love and allowing us our dignity and our right to pursue happiness.

This government that we live with would have us believe that we are all cared for equally. In truth, our government protects only itself and those with financial attractiveness. We have only to look on the streets to see that poverty, famine, and lost souls are everywhere while our political establishment feeds on caviar and champagne. We are the oxen the government uses to maintain its celebrity and its riches. The government is strong because it has built itself on the backs of slaves.

I have survived the worst. I was imprisoned, starved, beaten, and I lost the man I idolized most, my father. Yet, I am here to tell you that the human spirit cannot be *defeated by dictators, tyrants, and perpetrators of hate. There will always be those who feel they are above the laws of human decency. Those whose spiritual deficit would drag us into their cesspool of negativity. What we know of history is that there will always be men with deviant characters and treacherous natures waiting to jump on the discontent of others. Hateful souls that stir the dissatisfaction of the people into a murderous society where chaos reigns, tolerance has been buried, and spiritual demise is completed.*

But, do not lose hope, for there are still brave men and women who urge us to finally recognize that distinctions of culture, religion, and ethnic heritage are just perceptions of fear. They will encourage us to finally release those fears and turn our efforts to caring for one another. Only then can we conquer hate and realize that justice is more powerful than greed and that service and unconditional regard for one another is the only route to freedom. Only then can we, as citizens of the world, pursue that which we have been placed on this earth for, a productive life filled with love.

My fellow countrymen, I bid you farewell.

22 December 1978.

Galina's reading was followed by a silence so deep and profound that Katy knew Dimitri was there, smiling. His beloved wife had been reunited with his *ziechick*, and his writings had found a home. Galina went over to Elena and embraced her, and the two cried as Dimitri's spirit filled the room with love.

Katy stood and softly proposed, "I would like to make toast."

Andrei said, "Wait, Katy, I have a bottle of champagne that we can use to toast," and ran into the kitchen to retrieve it. He was back in no time with a tray of glasses filled with the bubbling liquid of the czars.

Katy stood again. "I have never known anyone like Dimitri. His life story is one of faith, determination, commitment to humanity, and love. I would like to make a toast to the bravest man I have ever met. May his spirit live on in all of us."

They lifted their glasses and said in unison, "To Dimitri." The clinking of their glasses sent out a harmonious vibration into the universe.

The night was finished with wine, laughter, and the renewing of bonds between mother and daughter and between friends. It ended with Andrei and Elena hosting Galina and Katy for the night.

As Elena was turning down their bed, Andrei brought over the envelope from Dimitri.

"You never opened the letter, Lena. Are you ready to now?"

Elena had almost forgotten about the sealed envelope inside the package that Dimitri had left her. The night she and Andrei shared looking at pictures she had tucked it away. Lena looked at him, hesitated for a moment, and then took the envelope. Opening the envelope and pulling out the letter from Dimitri, she read out loud to Andrei.

Moy ziechick,

I know I have caused you so much confusion and pain in your lifetime. Believe me, it was not my intent. You have been, and always will be, the light of my life. Sometimes, as parents we make decisions that oscillate the waves of time, and, eventually, the tsunami that is created catches up with us. When that happens, all we can do is ride out the wave and ask for forgiveness for our transgressions when what we have done causes our children such pain. I am an old man now, and, if there was any way I could go back and do this differently, I would. But of one thing I am sure. No matter what path I chose, it would have always included you at my side. You are the only person on this earth, besides your beautiful mother, who could be so strong. Strong enough to endure our difficult journey and come out the wonderful woman you have become. Your journey

*in this world is just beginning. Mine is nearly complete.
My father always told me that the most precious jewel
we can ever own is our family. I never doubted that good
man, and to this day I miss him terribly. So I will pass
this blessing along to you. May you always treasure those
who have come before you, those who are yours, and those
who will come after you. For they are your legacy, as you
are mine.*

*And by the way, Lena, open the door. Andrei is ready
to walk in if you let him.*

I love you, Ziechick.

Papa

Elena laughed through her tears and said, "Andrei, he knew all along that you were the one for me. But, he never said anything."

Andrei shrugged his shoulders. "I guess he thought you would figure it out, Lena." He cuddled up next to her. "And I'm so glad you did," he said as he kissed her forehead.

Elena smiled and allowed herself to be wrapped up in the love and contentment that she felt. As she was drifting off to sleep, she said, "Andrei, I think I have an idea for Katy."

"Really? Do you want to talk about it?"

"Not tonight. Let me sleep on it."

"OK, Lena, *Sladkiye sny*."[22] He brushed the hair back from her face as she fell asleep in his arms.

—

Elena awoke the next morning filled with a newfound energy. She was waiting with coffee when Katy descended the stairs.

"*Dobray ootra*, Katy."[23]

"Good morning, Lena, you're up early," Katy replied. "Big night last night, huh?"

"*Da*, I'm still blown away," Elena said, shaking her head as she offered Katy a cup.

"I can only imagine. I'm still in shock, too. It just happened so fast once I found her. But, you have your mother back."

"Katy, you have given me a second chance, one that I never thought I would have," Elena said, trying to hold back her tears. "You know, I know how much Papa thought of you. You were so good for him. He needed someone who could accept his crazy and be a captive audience for his stories," she said as she grabbed the creamer out of the refrigerator.

"We had some wonderful talks together. We did some healing together, too, and I really miss him," Katy said, pouring cream into her very black coffee.

---

22 Sweet dreams

23 "Good morning, Katy."

"Katy, I want you to know I got your letter. I never responded, but you should know I eventually, let go of my anger. Both of us were taken in by a man who was seriously disturbed."

"Lena, knowing what I know now, I can tell you Jack was mentally ill. I think he saw too much horror in his multiple deployments. The kind of trauma that Jack witnessed on a daily basis—no one could be unaffected by that. I think the Jack we knew was suffering terribly. He just didn't know how to deal with it or didn't realize it, I don't know which. But, I think he kept returning to the one place that made sense to him, the war. It was the one place where the outward chaos matched the inner chaos he was living with. The war was someplace he could hide his symptoms unnoticed, where all that macho hubris is lauded and supported. The troops were his accepting family, where he felt safe and where he didn't have to explain himself. He didn't know, Lena. He just didn't understand what was happening inside his head. I have thought so long and hard about the last time I saw him. I don't know this for sure, but the more I think about it, the more I think Jack didn't jump out of the helicopter to stop me from going into a minefield. I think he stepped out because he was done and it was the simplest way for him to end his torment. I don't know that for a fact, Elena, but it makes sense to me."

Heaving a huge sigh, Elena said, "You could very well be right. He was so troubled the last time he was home. Irrational, irritable, and almost insane with rage sometimes. There was no talking to him, and, to be honest, he had started to scare me." Elena looked at the floor and shook her head.

Katy reached over and took Elena's hand. "Well, Lena, I hope that he finally has some peace wherever he is now." She raised her cup to the ceiling.

"Me too, Katy, me too. Katy . . . I . . . umm . . . I had a crazy idea last night after I went to bed that I want to talk to you about. I'm not sure what your plans are, but what would you think about starting a wounded veterans dance program at the studio? I bet the VA would love to have something like that available to the troops, especially if they knew that someone who speaks the language of the military was behind the program. I could teach technique, and you could run the program. With your communication skills and contacts, I think we could make it a great success. It would be great to have you as an example of how dance technique can successfully help wounded veterans."

Katy looked at Lena in complete surprise. "Wow . . . Lena . . . I . . . I don't know what to say. I've booked a flight to go back to California to my parents. But . . . I really do need to finally get my life in order. It never occurred to me to stay here."

"Katy, it's perfect. Now that I say it out loud, I know it's perfect," Elena said with rising excitement. "Please just promise me that you will think about it. Please."

"It's so tempting, Lena. I think the two of us could rule the world," Katy said with a huge grin.

Elena smiled in agreement. "I really want you for this, Katy. We could honor those we have lost and provide a service to our vets."

The two women talked for another forty minutes, brainstorming ideas for the program. The more they talked, the more excitement they generated. When Andrei wandered into the kitchen and saw how animated the two of them were, he just turned around and went back to the living room to talk to Galena and introduce her to the twins. When they were through, Katy promised Elena she would return as soon as possible. After breakfast with her Russian family, Katy said tearful goodbyes to all.

With the shift in her relationship with Elena, Katy felt the promise of a new beginning, a new adventure, the something she had been searching for since she had arrived at Harbor Place all those months ago. *Life is strange, isn't it? Who would have thought that after losing my leg a year and a half ago, I would be running a dance program? Go figure.*

Smiling, Katy remembered her very first encounter at Harbor Place. "So I guess butterflies really do fly," she said out loud to herself.

She would be back in D.C. soon enough.

ACKNOWLEDGMENTS

So much has gone into this book, from the initial concept of writing this story, to trusting in the Universe that it would all work out. I started this project almost two years ago; I was able to write the story in about six months, but it turned out that was the easy part. I had two friends do a beta-read for me, and they both came back with great ideas and suggestions. But then I put the book away. Fortunately, the Universe continued to send me a little voice saying, publish your book. I finally listened and, when I did, everything fell into place.

The moment I met April O'Leary from O'Leary Publishing, I knew I was in good hands. April is the consummate businesswoman, and she and her team have not wasted a minute getting this book ready for publication. Heather Desrocher, assistant publisher and developmental editor, really helped pull the timeline of the story together. The cover design by Jessica Angerstein is flawless, and the copy editors, Hillary Sigale and Matthew Acton, put the finishing touches on all of it. I don't consider myself a very photogenic person, but Julie Renner's photos of me were so good that I actually had a hard time choosing the ones I liked the best. This team has supported me and helped see me through a process that I could never have undertaken without them. It has been so much fun learning how all of this comes together. I cannot express the enormous gratitude I have for their work on this book. I am looking forward to writing my next book with them—soon.

I am also grateful to my ballroom friends, Andrei and Elena Rudenco, who have taught me so much about the Russian culture and the lives of Russian people. Learning Russian history and some of the language has been a great side exercise as I have learned to dance. This book could not have been written without being privy to their stories of life in Eastern Europe.

On a different note, I am ever cognizant of the troubled times we are currently living in. It saddens me that we find it so difficult to learn from history. The warning signs are there, yet we turn our backs on what we know, dispute the truth, and find ways to be just as inhumane as we were some eighty years ago. But as wise Dimitri says in the story *"...do not lose hope, for there are still brave men and women who urge us to finally recognize that distinctions of culture, religion, and ethnic heritage are just perceptions of fear. They will encourage us to finally release those fears and turn our efforts to caring for one another."* It is my hope that this book will serve, in some small way, to change our current trajectory and will inspire us to turn our efforts to caring for one another.

May we always be grateful to those who have gone before us and for the lessons they have left behind.

Cathy Schaffer
Ft. Myers, FL
November 2019

BOOK CLUB QUESTIONS

Invite Cathy Schaffer to your Book Club! Cathy has limited spots each month to discuss Letters of Forgiveness via video conference with you and your friends. To book her please visit www. cathyschaffer.com and purchase the product "Book Club with Cathy". You'll be given instructions after purchase on how to secure your special date. Discussion can revolve around the questions below or any others you might want to suggest. She looks forward to seeing you soon!

1. Katy ultimately ends up with some of the same symptoms that Jack displayed. Does the fact that Katy's physical wound is so visible and Jack's wounds are so invisible, make her a more sympathetic character than Jack? Why or why not.

2. What are some of the subtler changes that occur in Katy's personality from the beginning of the book to the end?

3. Were you aware of the Russian Holocaust that occurred under Stalin's regime? Why don't we teach that in our world history classes?

4. Dimitri attributes his longevity and strength of character to the philosophical teachings that his father provided him as a young boy. What philosophical legacies are we leaving for our children?

5. Dimitri's last letter to his countrymen noting "*Those whose spiritual deficit would drag us into their cesspool of negativity. What we know of history is that there will always be men with deviant characters and treacherous natures waiting to jump on the discontent of others. Hateful souls that stir the dissatisfaction of the people into a murderous society where chaos reigns, tolerance has been buried, and spiritual demise is completed.*" This feels like a commentary about today's political climate. Do you agree or disagree and why?

6. He is also incredibly hopeful in his faith in mankind and says "*...do not lose hope, for there are still brave men and women who urge us to finally recognize that distinction of culture, religion, and ethnic heritage are just perceptions of fear.*" Who in our modern times fits this description in your opinion and why? Do you share his optimism?

7. What role does Elena's resentment towards her father play in her hurried marriage to Jack?

8. What similarities in personality do you see in Elena and Katy?

9. The cherry blossom tree finally drops its leaves at a pivotal
    point in the story – what do you think it represents?

10. The letters written by the characters in the book are based
    on self-reflection and a willingness to set ego aside and say
    "I'm sorry, I was wrong." Is there someone you need to write
    a "Letter of Forgiveness" to?

ABOUT THE AUTHOR

Cathy Schaffer was born in a small-town north of Syracuse, NY and spent most of her childhood living with her parents in Germany, where her father was stationed with the Air Force. Her childhood was difficult, due to her father's alcoholism and the resulting domestic violence that was a part of her home. Those years of violence and trauma led her to a career in healthcare.

Cathy was fortunate enough to graduate from Baylor College of Medicine in Houston, TX, where she raised her three children and became a Physician Assistant (PA). Her first job as a PA was working with women who were HIV positive. Cathy eventually went into critical care and heart surgery, a field where she has spent most of her career.

Cathy credits ballroom dancing for helping her discover self-confidence and balance in her life. For Cathy, "Ballroom dancing is a form of meditation that allows me to get in touch with my body and to focus my mind on the present moment." Cathy is a national award-winning competitive ballroom dancer who has participated in competitions across the country.

Cathy has always been a writer and still has the sixth-grade notebook where she wrote down observations about her teacher and classmates. Cathy is an avid journaler and has journals that are more than twenty years old. For her, "Journaling is like writing a letter to your best friend."

Not immune to the PTSD that comes from living in violence, Cathy has, through therapy and self-assessment, learned what it means to live with those memories and the emotional toll it takes. She has researched trauma extensively in order to understand how it affects the brain and the therapies that can help. Cathy is an advocate for those suffering with mental health issues and is the program coordinator for the Opioid Use Disorder Project at Lee Health in Fort Myers, FL.

Cathy lives in Fort Myers, FL, with her rescue toy poodle, Sadie, and continues to work full-time as a physician assistant. But, Cathy still finds time to practice her passions: dancing and writing.